THE MIDDLE CHILDREN

THE
MIDDLE
CHILDREN

BY
RAYDA JACOBS

CANADIAN CATALOGUING IN PUBLICATION DATA

Jacobs, Rayda
The middle children

ISBN 0-929005-59-7

I. Title.

PS8569.A36M5 1994   C813'.54   C94-931087-5
PR9199.3.J33M5 1994

Edited by Charis Wahl
Printed and bound in Canada

Second Story Press gratefully acknowledges the
assistance of the *Ontario Arts Council* and *The Canada Council*

Published by

SECOND STORY PRESS
760 Bathurst Street
Toronto, Ontario
M5S 2R6

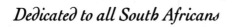

Dedicated to all South Africans

CONTENTS

ACKNOWLEDGEMENTS

To the Richvale Writers' Club for their encouragement and support, especially Bernice Farrar; to my editor, Charis Wahl; to Jan Daly for patiently reading the many rough drafts; to my sister for her invincible guardianship; to my daughter, Zaida, for listening to all the ideas, and to my son, Faramarz, for challenging every one of them; and, most of all, to my mother who has always encouraged me. Thank you, Mom.

I also wish to thank the Ontario Arts Council for its support.

❖

The recompense for an injury

is an injury equal thereto

(in degree): but if a person

Forgives and makes reconciliation

His reward is due

From Allah

(The Qur'an, 42:40)

THE MIDDLE CHILDREN

SMARTLY DRESSED in knee-high boots, mini skirt, Beatles jacket, and black beret, Sabah got off the bus at Mowbray station, and walked down the steps into the subway to the other side. Passing the thick knot of commuters who had bottled out of the bus to the far side of the platform where the first-class passengers would board, she was nervous, as always, expecting to hear her name called. The bus had loaded most of its fares in Athlone, and one day someone would shout her name, and the charade would end.

The two-minute wait for the train was the worst.

Turning to the crossword in the *Times*, she looked at the other travellers: the Carnaby girl with the op-art earrings chewing gum, the heavy-set Afrikaner with the folded *Burger*, the bell-bottomed hairdresser from Scissors 'n Things — South Africans were impressed by foreigners and she'd seen his picture advertised — and the other girl standing by herself at the far end of the platform.

The other girl was like herself. Not white, not black, but the offspring of many races: the neurotic middle child of a dysfunctional womb. She knew about the other girl as she knew the other girl knew about her. As a denture-wearer knows another plastic smile, an afflicted middle child can tell. From the stance, the wariness in the eyes. A middle child's constant fear was to be tapped on the shoulder and asked to go to the section reserved for non-whites.

The train arrived and she got on. Rocking gently in the green leather seat to the familiar rhythms of the carriage, blending in with the pressed suits, feeling safe, she returned to her anagrams. Then something made her look up. Stephanie van Niekerk from South Peninsula High! She hadn't seen Steffie since she took up with that German designer and moved into his flat in Green Point. Fair, with lots of freckles, sheets of raven black hair, Stephanie had a ballerina's prance, flicking her hair when she walked, middle as the day was long.

They got up from their seats and met near the door where there was standing room.

"Sabah!"

"Howzit?"

They were not suprised to find each other in this front section of the train.

"I heard you'd gone to Germany."

"I did. We came back."

"For good?"

"Yes. We live in Newlands now." Good old Newlands. Serene and green, and no hawkers allowed. "I'm still with Wolfie, you know."

"Really? That's a long time."

"And Laine's still with Joachim. They've got two kids now."

"And your other sisters? How many were there again?"

"Five. All married except for Janey who got divorced. And you? I don't see a ring."

"Ah, well."

"You're moving with the wrong crowd."

Sabah laughed.

"Get yourself a German or a Swede, Sabah. I'm telling you, you'll never go non-white again. They don't have that coloured mentality and they like dark. They come here because they're attracted to the exotic look." And she flicked her hair, smiling naughtily.

"Maybe if I was Christian I could."

"Could what?"

"You know, try white."

Stephanie laughed. "You still have those religious hang-ups?"

"Full of them, you don't know."

"Shame."

"Don't shame me, it's not that bad. I got engaged last year, but called it off."

"Really?"

"Yes. We were going to leave for Canada. I called it off, I can't leave. He's in Vancouver now."

"Shame."

"Stop it."

"Well, Wolfgang and I are also moving on. We want to start a family."

Sabah smiled. Stephanie's life had worked out. With a German husband, she'd have fair children, they'd attend a white school, and start out on the right foot. But could Stephanie escape who she was? Could you take a born-again pill with your Ovaltine and wake up someone else?

"You must come to the house. Wolfie has some terrific friends. Maybe you'll like Kurt. His English is a little stiff, but he's blond with blue eyes and a programmer with IBM. How about tomorrow night? We can meet under the clock and take the train home together after work. There're always people coming over, you never know who you can meet."

At Cape Town station she watched Stephanie in her strapless heels walk towards the foreshore, strangely curious at the prospect of Friday night. Would she be enticed? Envy Steffie's world? It was sure to be more exciting than hers. Things were easier as a Christian. You could fall in love, marry anyone. No rules, no duties, no fasting, no praying five times a day. She'd had a wild crush on a boy in Standard Six, Brian Dreyer, but even as a twelve-year-old knew it couldn't be, held back. And she wasn't anything like her friend. The first to smoke, experiment with sex, cross the colour line, Stephanie would laugh if she knew Sabah was still a virgin at twenty-one.

"A Sergeant van Schalkwyk's been calling for you," the receptionist said when she reached work. "He's with the C.I.D."

"The C.I.D.?" What would Criminal Investigations want with her? She went to her desk, and called the number.

"Miss Solomon," a heavily-accented voice said, "we'd like you to come down to Caledon Street police station this morning if you can."

"Is something wrong?" Her heart trilled like bongos in her chest.

"We have information that you're using a white card."

"What do you mean?"

There was irritation in his voice. "You were reported, we know you have a white card."

"Reported?"

"Can you come down this morning, please, or would you like us to come to where you work?"

Her father came with his lawyer, Jeffrey Fine, and met her outside the police station. He had a disappointed look, but didn't say anything. Her father refused to carry any card labelling him, and she had gone and obtained a white one.

But who would've reported her?

"Leave the talking to me," the lawyer said.

There were two of them, one with friendly eyes acting graciously, the other asking the pointed questions. The tea girl came in with a tray, and van Schalkwyk offered them a cup.

De Wet came straight to the point.

"It's a serious offence to obtain a white identification card if you're not white, Miss Solomon. You've also done so illegally."

The lawyer stepped in. "My client doesn't deny that she has a card. But we'd like you to take some things into account, why she did it. Sabah's a respectable girl from an educated family, white in appearance, and obtained the card because —"

"We're not talking about sitting in white restaurants or bioscopes, Mr. Fine. We can all see she can pass. She broke the law and we can't get away from that."

"There were no business schools five years ago for non-whites and Sabah obtained the card when she was sixteen to get into T.B.I. It was only a means to enhance her skills. And she's made something of herself. She's a legal assistant now. She knows what she's done's against the law, and has anxiety attacks worrying about being found out. She didn't get the card to be white, but for some of the small privileges we take for granted. It's not a crime, sergeant, to want to leap some of the hurdles in life."

"You're right, Mr. Fine, we're parents ourselves, we all want the best for our kids. But there're laws in this country, and we can't have people just helter skelter breaking the rules. Now, we understand that she's applied to Canada for a visa and has received one."

Her father interjected. "That was last year. She's not interested in emigrating anymore."

"So we're prepared to negotiate," van Schalkwyk continued as if no one had spoken. "The names of the people who supplied the card and she's free to leave the country. No charges will be brought. She has to be gone within a month."

"What?"

"That's the deal," de Wet said.

"But that's outrageous!"

"Life's outrageous, Mr. Fine. We're being generous. The names of the people or organization who supplied the card and gone by the end of next month. It's not that we don't want her in South Africa, South Africa belongs to all of us, but if she's not here when we make the arrests, we can't put her in jail, can we?"

Fine talked back and forth for two hours, but it was like pissing into the Augrabies Falls.

Van Schalkwyk closed the file and got up. "We'll leave you for a few minutes to sort yourselves out."

Fine convinced his clients that the Security Police were not to be confused with, to use an American expression, the palookas investigating a b and e, and would hold on to their prey like hyenas till the end. She would be made an example of, her picture would appear in the papers, and there was the possibility of jail. Was Canada not worth a try? He himself had friends there, who reported a better life. It was a chance.

De Wet and van Schalkwyk returned, and Fine made a last desperate plea. The sergeants sat unmoving as the Drakensberg. With the cold speed of a bank transaction, the name of the contact — deceased two years previously — was given, and Sabah was released.

On a dismal day in May, her mother's crimplene dress a white dot on the dock, Table Mountain bid her a silent, majestic goodbye. The wind whipped at her hair and she sank down between the passengers and cried into her hands.

❖

Masquerade

THE RAIN DRIPPED from the roof of the stoep, sparkling like crystal studs on the leaves of the hanging vine. For a moment she fastened onto these cellophane drops in a winter sky, promising hope, tomorrow, when the darkness would lift and everything would be gone: the bier with its red satin dome, the silent, bleak-eyed women grating camphor in the living room, the sickly sweet smell of day-old corpse mingled with dried rose leaves and condensed-milk tea, the lorry waiting to take the cottonwool-packed body to the mosque.

Where was her mother?

She saw the birds gliding in a vee over the house. Something squeezed in her chest, she couldn't breathe. She was cold with two jerseys on and had to pee but was afraid to go to the toilet. He had fallen in there. First the cup from his hand into the terrazzo tub, then him on the tiled floor. Dead as they carried him down the hall. The house felt as if something lived in the walls: clammy, threatening, waiting for her in the passage to reach its dank hand into her neck.

No one else was on the stoep. Should she peer in? The curtain wasn't drawn all the way. No, she would be sick, like the time she'd been forced by Miss van Graan to go to a Christian boy's funeral. The marble face with the spittle on the blue lips. And that smell. The body had been in that small room two days and, in the heat, the rot had clung to her school *gym*, threatening to bring her breakfast to her throat. She could still see the old lady with the rolled-up newspaper swatting at the flies.

But she was curious. Four *toekamandies* had gone in. What were they doing in there? What was a heart attack? Looking sideways without turning her head, she backed closer to the window, collecting her strength. Turning slowly, she pushed her forehead into the pane. It took a few moments for her eyes to adjust to the body on the *kateel*, a metal table with a drain, a bath underneath catching the water trickling down. A white sheet covered the corpse, men, their hands wrapped in white cloths, positioned at the head, feet, arms, washing the body under the sheet. Then one of them lifted a foot and she saw the stiff leg move. It chilled her. A dead body in there! He wasn't going to be at the supper table with Oemie and her mother any more. No longer would that ruler be pointed at her nose for her to keep quiet while he read. He was going to another home, cold and wet. The angels would come, the sand walls squeezing him if he'd sinned.

"Hey, what you doing looking in dere!"

She turned at her aunt's voice and ran from the stoep into the rain. The owls would come tonight. They'd come for three nights, and her grandfather had died. They should be satisfied now. It was time for them to sit in other trees, warning other people.

Someone loaded her onto the lorry with twelve other kids. Girls were not allowed in cemeteries. Maybe she

looked like a boy with this new haircut her mother had
given her. "Don' still make frills 'n drills with dat hair,"
her grandmother had said. "Soon she mus' wear a scarf.
An' she's six awready, why you let her wear pants?"

The earth was red, gravelly, wet. Two men in the hole.
One positioning the body facing east, the other fitting the
planks. Wedged tight in his cave, his roof at right angles
over his head to wait for Judgement Day. For the angels
to come and ask what good he had done and testify
against him if he lied. Would the linen come loose and the
sand drop on his face? How long would it take for the
skin to crawl with that other life? Would they curl
through his eyes like caterpillars or come slithering
through his mouth?

What if his soul *hadn't* left through his collarbone like
the Book said, and he was shouting with unmoving lips
that he was alive?

And felt the sand coming down?!

"Make sure you're wearing clean panties, you're going
with Moena and Juleikha to the calipha's house,"
Kareema said.

"Why?" Sabah asked her aunt. She'd been at her
aunt's three days now while her parents sorted out their
troubles, and wished it was suppertime already when her
mother would pick her up. All her mother's sisters, especially Auntie Kareema, were against her father. Auntie
Shamila wasn't bad, she sometimes joked with her father,
and the two of them would laugh, but Auntie Kareema
and Auntie Zanap didn't like her father and didn't like
her because she looked like him. "White Fiekie," they
called him — Fiekie for Shafik. Still, it was better here

than at Auntie Zanap's next door where all the boys called her names.

"You can't send her without Aisa's permission," Shamila said.

"Those women are only there today. You know they don't do it openly any more."

"They shouldn't be doing it at all. And it's not your business to send Sabah."

"They don't really do anything, they just look."

"It's not your child. And you know they don't just look."

"We went, didn't we, when we were kids, and it didn't do us any harm?"

"You went, not me. Anyway, it's wrong and has nothing to do with God. It's something men came up with to keep women under control. Because they can't control themselves, they think no one can, and doing this will tame us like yard cats who have been fixed."

"Ya Allah, Shamila, watch your mouth," Kareema wiped at the perspiration on her face with her scarf. "It's wrong to speak like that. You want to be cursed?"

"Why must I go, Auntie?" Sabah asked again.

"You ask too many questions. Run along."

Sabah felt a finger of pain and slowly reversed out the room. Why hadn't her mother sent her instead to her grandfather's house where you played all day and went out with a flask of coffee and sandwiches with Swart Piet and the cows? They were too mean in this house, too strict. Did God want them to be so frightened of Him?

Shamila looked briefly in her direction, then put her foot down on the treadle making the machine sing. Sabah liked the *ðtzz ðtzz ðtzz* that it made. Her mother at the sewing machine. The time when her father was gone for

a week and she ran constantly into the house to check
that her mother hadn't left too. When she heard the cup
rock in the saucer, she relaxed. She didn't feel safe in this
house. With seven boys next door calling her "white
bread" in front of her friends, and her Granpa Doels with
the beige Peugeot and those wonderful comic books
living so far away.

"Let's go," Moena said, taking a shiny sixpence out of
her pocket. "We have money for stars."

"We can go to Abassie's on our way."

"Okay."

"Here's some toffee rolls," Auntie Shamila said, reaching into her bag. "Don't make yourselves all sticky and
come straight home, you hear?"

It was a three-mile walk to the white-plastered house
next to the mosque, and the girls wasted all kinds of time
in the store deciding between gumballs, stars and lucky
stripes. Sabah had left her toffee roll behind for that
evening when she would read, for the third time, the new
book with the glossy pages Granpa Doels had dropped
off for her, and took out her sixpence to contribute to the
pool. Her mother didn't know of the two shillings she
had in her drawer that Granpa Doels had given her when
he showed up at school with Cadbury bars for her and
her friends. He did things like that. Like the time when
she was three and he bought her a pony and named it
Masquerade, then started to call her that. "Come here,
my little Masquerade, read your ol' Granpa a story." And
she would lift the big book with the shiny cover to her
knees and throw in some big words she'd heard on the
radio. Her grandfather's laughter would reach all the way
back in his throat and he'd go to the kitchen and whip
them up bowls of black berries with clotted cream. Or

the time he invited her friends to stay with her at the farm during the school holidays and took them all to the gymkhana at Kenilworth and to the bioscope afterwards. She wished she could stay there for good.

By the time they reached the calipha's house their faces were purple and pink, hands sticky, shoes scuffed from kicking pebbles and cans in the *sluits*.

"I'm scared."

"Sheeda said it doesn't hurt."

"They take off your panties," Moena said.

Julaikha giggled, and Sabah reminded herself that she wasn't wearing her navy blue knickers, but the white nylon ones with the lace.

"Why?"

"They tickle you."

"They don't tickle you, stupid. There's blood."

"Blood?!"

They stood at the gate looking up at the crowded stoep, the young girls wearing scarves, a woman in a black veil walking around with a plate.

"Is it a party?"

"They give you cake afterwards. Look, there's Soda. Let's go talk to her."

"I'm not going," Sabah said.

"You'll get a hiding if you don't."

"Your mother can't hit me, I'll tell."

The woman with the cake plate waved them in.

On the stoep Sabah felt herself pressed in on all sides by girls pushing anxiously to go through the door into the house as if Father Christmas was on the other side. The ones coming out had a strange look — not pain — and some of them even smiled, as if they'd just passed, with great difficulty, some important test. Friends would

huddle around, and the girl would lift up her dress and
peer at her panties underneath. There would be whisper-
ing, giggling, the lady with the plate bringing tarts and
ginger beer, everyone congratulating the girl as if she'd
run the mile.

"Did it hurt?" Moena asked Soda.

"No. Just a little prick."

"Can we see the blood?"

"There's no blood."

"See? I told you," Moena said.

She was in the living room now, fourth from the bedroom door. Why was she there, when did these choky
feelings start? At Oupa's funeral, or the time he told her
father not to put his foot in the house again? She remembered it still. In bed in the front room, her father on the
stoep coming to take her mother back, Oupa saying no.
She'd heard it all through the window, how he asked her
father to leave, her father's footsteps on the cement, the
car starting up, the engine dying away down the street.

Smiling at her cousins behind her, her heart fluttering
like a robin with clipped wings, she lost her breath and
passed out. When she opened her eyes, she was on a
table in hell with a light dangling over her legs, petrified
by the black-veiled women holding her down, reaching
under her dress; silent, toothless hags, reminding her of
those birds with the long beaks sitting on dead animals in
the bush.

She opened her mouth to scream, but nothing came
out.

"Lookit de birdie," one of them said, motioning to the
fly-specked bulb overhead.

Sabah squeezed her knees together, but they were
wrenched apart, and she felt the clammy hands with

something cold between her thighs. Then a sudden savageness rose in her breast. God didn't want this! She wrenched her legs free, kicking at breasts and robes, knocking instruments to the floor. Six hands shot out, but the poison inside her swelled and she heard a savage scream pass her lips. Then she was at the door, cutting through incense and eau de cologne, snot catching in her hair, feet barely touching the asphalt.

Her mother had arrived to pick her up, and was in the kitchen drinking tea with her aunts. Charging by them to the back of the house, Sabah shot them venomous looks.

"Can't you greet? Even a dog barks," Kareema said. "And where's Moena and Julie?"

"No, I CAN'T!! AND I WON'T!!"

The women looked at one another, alarmed. Her mother came to the bathroom door.

"Sabah? What's wrong, my girl? What happened? Where were you?"

Inside the porcelain room she turned on the tap in the bath and sat shivering on its edge. Her thighs were sticky and warm and, on her knee, a red tear sat in the groove of her skin. When she finally looked, she cried soundlessly into the hem of her dress to find her panties still there, dry, and that whatever it was had only nicked the inside of her leg.

❖

MISS PRETORIOUS

MRS. VERKEER WAS IN THE KITCHEN peeling potatoes for supper, listening to the radio, when her serial was interrupted for the news.

This is a special bulletin. Prime Minister Verwoerd was stabbed to death today during a parliamentary session in the House of Assembly ...

The potato dropped into the sink, and she looked at the radio as if it could confirm that she'd heard right. Hendrik Verwoerd? The country's most rigid and forceful practitioner of apartheid? Dead?! Whaaahh *ghottala* ... and she ran out of the house, not sure what to do, who to share the news with. Would old Mr. Lewenberg next door have heard? Maybe he was sitting on the stoep and didn't know. She got to the gate, wiping her wet hands on her apron, and spotted Mrs. Prins across the road bending down in her garden. She wouldn't speak to that Nosy Parker and quickly turned back inside. Would Evvy know? Of course, she would. They played radios in offices now. She would call her daughter at work. Being in the heart of town, Evvy would know more. She was proud of her daughter, her good job as a typist for architects. Still unmarried at twenty-nine. Mrs. Verkeer had immense faith that soon the Lord would send the right man for Evelyn. She dialled the number, wondering what her tenant would feel, knowing what she knew of the young history teacher. The cheek of the girl. The audacity. Did Miss Pretorious have no shame?

The following day, still shaken from the news, the school-teacher could tell from the vibration in the classroom that little time would be devoted to lessons that afternoon. Cape Town rocked with the news. The assassination provoked international cries of dismay. World leaders opposed to apartheid still deplored his death.

"Good morning, Miss Pretorious."

"Good morning, class. Please sit down."

Her top student put up his hand.

"We'd like your opinion on the assassination, Miss Pretorious."

"I don't deal in opinions, Ivan. The fact is, we lost a prime minister last night."

"YESS!!"

She ignored that. "Clive?"

"Do you think that whoever gets to be elected now will be more liberal than Verwoerd?"

"We're in the world spotlight, who knows?"

"I mean he got it good in the neck. They should start watching their backs."

The whistling and desk-banging was deafening.

"Class!"

"We've been centre stage before, what's new about that? We don't need a Winds-of-Change speech," Ivan continued, "we need some serious arse-kicking *bringing* change!"

The noise flared up again, and the teacher banged on her table with a book.

"You're out of order, all of you." But there was amusement in her eyes. "I'm leaving this class for five minutes. When I return I want you turned to page a hundred and nine."

She walked briskly to the staff toilets, taking a swallow of water from one of the taps. The overhead mirror showed a young woman with a blush complexion — a Cape Town euphemism for not quite dark — broad nostrils, pretty eyes, kinky hair straightened into a stiff bouffant. Miss Pretorious would not be mistaken for white. Miss Pretorious didn't want to be white. But Miss Pretorious had a secret that made her sweat at nights. What would her parents say? Her students, if they knew? The face in the mirror shouted, hypocrite.

Her parents were out in the Cape Flats, but she lived in the renovated servants' quarters of Margaret Verkeer, a Seventh Day Adventist, and her sour daughter, Evelyn. Sometimes the old girl would come and have tea with her in the small kitchen and she'd help her fill out forms Mrs. Verkeer didn't want Evelyn to know about and, often a plate of pineapple fritters waited for her on the kitchen sill at the back. Yesterday a note with a single request was under the door.

Shortly after midnight, in bed, charged with the words of the Lord, Mrs. Verkeer didn't have to hear the hinge on the gate to know the lover had arrived. She was familiar with the engine sounds of the taxi and, in the moonlit room, his shadow danced on the wall as he catfooted past her window down the cement path to the back. At dawn the same taxi whisked him out of the neighbourhood. How could Miss Pretorious do this to them? What if anyone were to look out their window and see? Especially that Mrs. Prins? It would be all over the neighbourhood: a white man coming out of Margaret Verkeer's house! Tomorrow she would have a word with Miss Pretorious.

But the next day the man from the Municipality came — they'd heard there were servants' quarters not shown on the building plans — and Mrs. Verkeer was busy mollifying him with pancakes and tea, forgetting all about her talk with Miss Pretorious. The teacher didn't respond to her landlady's request, so it was Wednesday before Mrs. Verkeer, seeing the glow of the kitchen light on the guava tree in the yard, quickly took herself to the back.

"Miss Pretorious," she caught the teacher in the middle of supper, "I've got to talk to you about something that's been on my mind. In a way it's none of my business, but then it also is. What I mean, is —"

"Is it about Michael?"

"Michael?"

"My fiancé."

"He's your fiancé?"

"We're getting married in December, yes. I was going to come and talk to Mrs. Verkeer and give notice at the end of the month."

The air went out of Mrs. Verkeer like a slow puncture.

"Married? You and him?"

"And as Mrs. Verkeer knows, we can't live here in South Africa until they scrap the Act. So we're moving to Bechuanaland in the new year. I hope Mrs. Verkeer understands."

"Well, that's a horse with a different colour, isn't it? Marriage. I see. I mean, it's only because of the neighbours, you understand. The law. I mean, I don't mind, but if word gets out, you know how spiteful people can be."

"Michael and I don't want trouble. He likes this country, coming from such a damp place as England, but we have no choice now but to leave, as if being in love is a crime."

Vaguely aware of the apple spice aroma drifting out of the stove, Mrs. Verkeer tried hard for a smile. To her, it *was* a crime. That flatnosed Miss Pretorious with her kaffir hair and Bushman lips breaking God's Commandments could land a man, a white one — good-looking, well-dressed — and her church-going daughter with green eyes and straight hair couldn't find anyone. Where was the justice in that? What did this *platkop* have? Besides lifting up her skirt for a man?

"I'm sorry if I've caused Mrs. Verkeer any worry, but I can't say enough how relieved I am that it's finally out."

"And your family? They don't know about him?"

"Not yet. My father has a bad heart, he won't take it well."

In her own kitchen Evelyn had just cleared away the supper dishes and made a pot of tea.

"You mean that girl brought someone here all the time, right under our noses, a white man, while we were asleep? How disgusting, ma! And you only tell me now?"

"Can you imagine if Mrs. Prins should look out her window and see?"

"The whole world will know. Did you get a look at him? What's he look like?"

"Nothing much," Mrs. Verkeer lied.

"She's trouble, ma, let her go. We won't have trouble finding a good tenant."

"She's leaving at the end of the year. And she promised

he would only come weekends now."

"What? How can you let it go on? What if people find out? And you're allowing sin on the premises."

"But Evvy, can you believe it? Marriage? I wouldn't have thought it of her."

"It's the quiet ones that bite in the dark. Get rid of her, ma, let her go."

Walking home from church that Saturday, Mrs. Verkeer came around the corner of her street and too late saw Mrs. Prins catapult herself from her gate. "I hear you gotta midnight visitor dese days."

"Me?"

"Lewenberg says he hears de gate at night."

She'd thought the old man was asleep by nine.

"A white man comes to your teacher in de back. With a taxi. In de middle of de night."

Mrs. Verkeer took a handkerchief from her clutch bag and dabbed at her face. "My own little Miss Pretorious, are you sure? She's such a decent girl."

"You mean you don't know what goes on in your yard?"

"I'm asleep by ten, Mrs. Prins."

"You heard what happened to Hettie's son, didn't you? A Portegies living with dat loafer of hers in de back and dey came in de middle of de night. At three a clock when even God's taking a nap. Dat's when dey come, you know. Bang downa door an' charge in like animals an' wake de whole neighbourhood up, dragging dem out by deir necks an' keeping dem ninety days under de Act, troo's Gawd."

Sweat pearls formed in the groove above Mrs. Verkeer's upper lip.

"People are spiteful, man," Mrs. Prins continued.

"Troo friends is stranger dan sunshine in June."

Mrs. Verkeer found the teacher sunning herself in the yard. "I just ran into Mrs. Prins, the biggest busybody in Athlone. She tells me everyone knows what's going on."

"But how? Michael only comes Saturday nights."

"She says old Lewenberg next door hears the gate, but I think it's her." Mrs. Verkeer pulled at the weeds between the geraniums. "I know I said you could stay till the end of the year and I haven't changed my mind, but people are sitting at their windows with binoculars now. I must ask you not to let him come to the house anymore. Is that a terrible thing to ask?"

"No problem, Mrs. Verkeer," Miss Pretorious tucked at her floral wrap. "We only have a few weeks anyway."

"Thank you. I'm sorry, but you know how it is."

"I understand, Mrs. Verkeer."

The taxi stopped coming and the weeks passed. When Mrs. Verkeer ran into Mrs. Prins again the focus was on Fatima Bowler whose teenage daughter's pregnancy had just come to light, the girl's pleas not to marry causing uncles to descend like prophets from the four corners of the Cape, quoting haphazardly from the Qur'an. After a quick-fix by Imam Hosein, tea and coconut tarts, the girl was married to a carpenter she'd only dated twice. These fast-talking mozzies with their fancy cars, shooting their seed, marrying to make it right, and now exposing their tools under steering wheels of Buicks on Signal Hill.

On New Year's Eve the cars lined up outside the house as people came to say goodbye to the teacher. Listening to the music and laughter, Mrs. Verkeer felt strangely out of sorts. Something nagged at her. She felt the same uneasiness as the time she'd dozed off on that hot afternoon when Willie was ill, had a dream that he was floating face down in the Liesbeek, and found him dead of a heart attack in the bath the next day.

At eleven she decided not to wait up for Evelyn and went to bed. The stress of the last few months had been too much. Still, Evelyn could've gone to the back and wished the teacher well. It cost nothing to be nice, and it took courage to put your life in a suitcase and leave. South Africa, for all its *krake* was home — *she'd* never leave, even if the blacks took charge. The girl could write a clever letter, had indeed saved her from the Municipality, and always had time to do you a turn. Perhaps it was that Miss Pretorious was more decent than some of those starched virgins hallelujahing it up in church that weighed so heavily on her mind.

Somewhere around four, when the night was still and you could hear the devil breathe, she came out of a fitful sleep. Was it the gate? Something in the next room? She watched the trees sway like dinosaurs on the bedroom wall and tried to pinpoint where the sound had come from. But nothing moved. A cough on the other side of the wall reassured her Evelyn was home. Maybe it was her daughter coming in or going to the bathroom that had woken her up. But the uneasiness squeezed at her chest and she recognized that feeling of doom.

The curtains stirred in the breeze, her heart picked up a beat, and in the distance she felt them approach. Silent as serpents, then the screeching brakes, voices barking through the front door.

❖

MADULA

THE HOLE WAS IN THE MIDDLE of the yard, between the stables and the chicken run. She knew the diggers: crippled Cupido, who lived in Mr. Hennie's shed on the other side of the soccer field, and his pal, Dhol. Swart Piet was too old and arthritic to climb in and dig, although he was in charge, every so often jerking his head, swearing at something on his right shoulder, laughing for no reason at all.

Dullah, in long rubber boots, khaki hat and shorts, a cigarette behind his ear, stood with Swart Piet looking down at the diggers as the shovels kicked into the pit, scooped, depositing huge mounds at their feet.

She walked up gingerly.

"Granpa Doels?"

His smile faded.

"What're you doing out this early? And without your gown and shoes?"

"I wanted to see."

"It's winter, you'll catch cold. Now go inside before Little Granny whacks your bum."

"Granpa?"

"Yes?"

"Can Christian people dig the hole for the Qorban?"

"It doesn't matter who digs the hole; it's the deed that counts. God accepts everyone's good work."

She was silent for a moment, squinching her toes in the wet grass. It looked like no good deed to her. She had tossed all night thinking about how Madula would die. Would she snort and kick her heels in the dust, refusing to come to the hole? Would she feel the cold steel of the knife? Would she die right away and not feel anything? A faint drizzle touched her cheek and she wished the skies would open up and drown everything out and her grandfather would have to cancel the Qorban.

"I think He's a selfish God."

He turned, surprised, but she was already walking back to the house.

Swart Piet cackled as he relit a half-smoked cigarette, shouting down to Dhol not to throw sand on his feet.

"Dat Cookie's a Solomon awright."

Dullah smiled.

"Okay, that's deep enough."

The boys handed up their shovels, and climbed out.

Swart Piet fitted the wide plank over the hole, knocking each end into the earth with his cracked boot.

"Good job, Cupido, thank you," Dullah said, handing them each ten shillings. "Don't forget to come by this afternoon for your meat."

They nodded their thanks, and Cupido took off his hat, scrunching it unconsciously in his hands where he held it over his crotch.

"*As baas vir my die kop kan hou, asseblief?* If it's not too forward to ask?"

Dullah was a novelty to his Christian neighbours. Owning race horses, cattle, he went to the track, threw jazz parties on New Year's Eve, and wasn't like any Muslim they knew. He turned a blind eye to workers throwing dice, but drew the line at liquor on his premises. He gave generously to anyone who asked. It was his contention that it didn't matter whether the beggar was in rags or in silk. If he asked, he didn't have, and the onus was on him, God said, to give. People knocked on his door for food, odd jobs, loans, and he often created projects, upsetting his snappy little wife who still raged over the crooked brick barbecue a gardener thought he could build.

"Old Madula's head? Of course. I'll save it for you. Not many takers for brains and eyes, although my wife likes the tongue. Makes a good roast. Fried brains and onions can taste just like omelette."

Cupido didn't know what omelette was and smacked the hat on his head, showing a nicotine smile.

"Dankie baas."

"Don't call me baas, Cupido."

"Okay, baas."

Janey was in the kitchen, slapping her hands into dough. He could tell by the ridge between her eyes that panic was setting in. It was just after seven and, by noon, a hundred guests would cram into the house and yard for the Eid festivities. Her sisters were due to help with the breyani and curry, but he knew from her mutterings she would still primp and fuss even though the meat had all been prepared, marinating in green coriander and yogurt overnight, puddings and trifles and mince pies still to arrive from his brother's house.

"Piet knows what to do outside. I need some help in here."

"Why you making roeties, my *bok*? It's too much work,

man, there's rice."

"Roetie tastes better with lamb curry. Can you put out the ginger beer on the stoep?"

"Where's Sabah?"

"Inside. She came in with wet feet mumbling about something. Her mother's coming to pick her up. We don't want any performances. And make sure she's wearing warm clothes. Don't let her catch cold on her last day and we get the blame."

"What's for breakfast?"

She shot him a look.

"And don't still bother with eggs or anything fancy. There'll be no place in this kitchen in half an hour."

Her long hair was twisted into a bun at the back of her head, and he came up, pulling out two of the pins.

"Stop it."

He pulled out the last one, watching the coil jump down her back, and quickly escaped into the front bedroom where Sabah was rummaging through her suitcase.

"And what's my little Masquerade wearing today?"

She held out her plum corduroy pants.

"That? There'll be girls here in sequins and pearls. Your cousins, too. Don't you want to be the prettiest? What about that nice green velvet dress with the lace your mommy made?" And he slipped in what had to be said, "You know she's coming today."

"I don't want to go home, Granpa."

"It's school tomorrow, my girl. You promised her you wouldn't carry on like the last time."

"I can live here with you and Little Granny. You can drive me to school."

"Your mommy will miss you. She misses you already when you come for the holidays."

"She won't miss me, she has Oemie. I don't like it there. With Auntie Kareema and my other cousins next door."

"You've been here for three weeks."

"And my daddy? Will he miss me when I'm gone?"

"Of course."

"I don't think he likes little girls."

"Why do you say that?"

"He never asks if I want to come with him in the car, or anything. And mommy says I come here for him. You remember my friend, Shirley? Her father takes her to ballet lessons every Saturday. And when I go there, he takes us to the park. Even though the park's right at the back of the house." She paused to pick at the lint on her nightdress. "I want a daddy like other people, Granpa. My friends don't believe I have one. They say I made him up."

"Where do they think you came from then? The wind?"

She searched around for her socks, a serious look on her face.

"Can you have children, Granpa, without a husband?"

"Of course you can," he laughed. "You can have anything you want if you put your mind to it."

"Anything?"

"Anything. If it sits in your heart long enough, you get it. But be careful what you wish for."

"Why?"

"Because not everything you wish for is good for you. Only God sees around the bend. Now, what were you saying about God outside?"

"I said He's a selfish God. Why does He want us to kill Madula for Him?"

"He doesn't want Madula. You know the story of the Sacrifice. It's to remember what Abraham did."

"But it was cruel of God to expect him to sacrifice his son. Would you do it, Granpa, if you had a vision from God?"

"Maybe that's why I don't have children. God knows I'm weak. And Abraham didn't have to do it, remember? At the last minute the lamb came."

"But what if the lamb *didn't* come, Granpa, and Abraham really sacrificed his son?"

"But it didn't happen that way, did it? It was a test for Abraham and he passed it. He didn't question God's will. And, when he told his son what he had to do, his son agreed. Abraham listened to God. And the son listened to his father. There should be a story about little girls listening to their grandfathers."

"Don't be funny, Granpa."

He laughed, biting her on the cheek. "Go and brush your teeth, I'll put out your clothes. You can wear your corduroy pants until the people come, then change into your dress. And be careful you don't get it dirty and wet."

"I still don't see why Madula should die. Can't you just buy meat from the butcher for the people? She isn't a regular cow. She understands Swart Piet and gives us milk every day."

"Exactly. In desert countries camels carry loads, give milk, and their hair can also be woven into cloth. Cows and goats and sheep are useful to us. When they're sacrificed, though, we show that we're willing to give up some of our own benefits for others. Not everyone goes to bed with a full stomach like us. Muslims have a chance to give thanks and celebrate the Sacrifice of Abraham and Isma'il on the tenth of *Dhu al Hijjah*."

"But why must *you* do it, Granpa? Mommy says you already give sadakah."

"Because God gave me a lot. It isn't enough just to give a few pounds of rice during Ramadan, you have to give any time someone asks. *And*," he smiled, "a man with my many sins must do some things right."

"Being a Muslim is hard, Granpa. God wants too many things. Look at how many times He wants us to pray. Shirley only prays on Sundays. And then she gets to wear a new dress."

She watched with two cousins from Masquerade's stall as her grandfather, Imam Hosein with his white robe and headgear threaded with gold, and uncles and nephews and friends came from the kitchen into the yard.

Swart Piet had removed Madula's bell — the bell that had so aggravated Mr. Pietersen down the street — lightly tying a rope around her neck, the free end attached to the loquat tree at the side of the house. It had all been unnecessary. Madula was resting under the tree, her huge eyes sad and grey. There was about her a silence and peace, as if she knew.

Swart Piet talked to her in that rumbling way he had, rubbing her flank, and wrapped a cloth loosely around the head, covering her eyes. Tugging gently on the rope, Madula followed him to the pit.

There was a murmur in the crowd when they saw the blindfolded cow. This wasn't how it was done.

Testing the thick plank over the hole with his foot, Swart Piet tapped Madula on the flank, and the cow buckled its forelegs and went down, her head inches away from the pit.

"Let's go stand near the hole," Gadidja said. "I want to see."

"Yes. It smells in here," her sister, Sadia, agreed. "Look at my shoes."

"I'm staying," Sabah said, her patent leathers rimmed with manure.

"*Heeretjie*, look at Karnita's hair. Do you think she puts stuff on it to make it so red?"

"No. They all look like that, like they were dipped in Rooibos tea."

The others laughed, and someone shouted for them to keep quiet.

"Isn't your father helping Granpa Doels slaughter the cow?" Gadidja asked.

"I don't know."

Behind them Masquerade dropped a load. They wrinkled their noses in unison.

"Our clothes are gonna stink."

"Granpa Doels isn't his father," Sadia said.

"Whose father?"

"My mother says Granpa Doels isn't your father's real father."

"She's a liar! Granpa Doels *is*!"

"She's not a liar!"

"She doesn't know anything, she's stupid! She works in a fish factory!"

"But she didn't marry a half *naartjie*, did she? Can't you see with your own eyes? Your father's white, your grandfather's a chocolate cone!"

"My father's *not* a half *naartjie*! And my grandfather *isn't* chocolate!"

"*Bismilla Hiragman Niraghim*," the Imam started.

"And, he has a girlfriend!"

Three men manouevred the cow on its side, and Swart
Piet pulled on the rope to get her head on the plank.
When she was down, Dullah took a rag from his pocket
and soaked it with chloroform.

"My friend ...," the Imam started. "We can't ..."

"It's a small mercy to the animal, Imam." And he
applied the wet cloth over the cow's nostrils and mouth.

The men behind him sucked in their breaths. Dullah
played by his own rules, but this was way out of line. It
was a mockery and might even contaminate the meat.

"A girlfriend?"

"Yes. Your father has a girlfriend! That's why your
mother left! She found out!"

Sabah punched her in the face. "It's not true!"

"Fiekie play too much with his dickie, everyone says!"

Sabah punched her again.

Sadia's glasses fell off and she fell flat on her arse in
the hot shit.

"Call your mother now, four eyes!" Sabah kicked
Sadia as Gadidja opened her mouth to scream.

The Imam started the prayer, Swart Piet tightened the
rope. Dullah flicked the knife once, cutting quickly into
the vein. The blood surged out in a thick spurt and hit
him in the leg. The onlookers watched in silence as the
convulsing animal jerked, then came slowly to rest on the
plank.

Sabah was on Sadia's chest hammering with her fists
when Little Granny's wooden spoon lit into her behind.
Next to her grandmother, disappointment thick on his
face, stood Granpa Doels, blood on his hands, in stained
pants, slowly nodding his head.

❖

BOUNDARIES

WHITE-TILED, MONITORS, TUBES, MACHINES. Clotted blood in tangled hair.

"I'm Dr. Carvainis, the neurosurgeon. Are you the sister? You don't have to come in if it frightens you."

"Yes, Erica Preston."

"The CT scan showed a small hematoma. We won't operate at this time."

"Will she survive?"

"It's too early to tell. The brain will swell first — she's received a severe blow to the head — then as it subsides we hope she'll come out. It's like a bowl of jelly that's dropped to the floor. It's not quite out of the bowl, but everything's shifted around."

It was someone else's nightmare. Quiet, hushed, nurses gliding like ghosts down dim corridors. How had she gotten there? Where could she sit down and think? The policeman had brought her, asking questions about Lionel. Was there a slab with her sister's name waiting somewhere?

"And — the man she was with?"

"He didn't survive the attack."

She went home for a few hours' sleep and woke up when her eldest sister, Rose, arrived from Port Elizabeth.

"She shouldn't have been born, that would've been best. Or with two heads. A little vamp she was, even in diapers, my father laying off band practice for more than a year coming straight home from work to put her to bed himself. Her colour I could understand. My mother's father was white, you know, and my parents weren't unattractive people, there was straight hair in the family. But no one looked like her, so fine-featured and fair.

"Christmas was the worst time because all the aunties came, and it didn't matter how my hair was ribboned or rolled, how I shone in my taffeta, she could come in with her dress hanging by a thread, I would become as important as wallpaper. She'd get the biggest doll, the best books, more cream on her strawberries than Rose and me. It took years to figure out why I always started the new year depressed."

"And your eldest sister?"

"Nothing affects Rose. Rose put on thirty pounds when she was ten and never lost it. At eighteen she married a bank teller and moved to P.E. She's content being a housewife, driving her children to Bible class. She's the happy one."

"And you became a teacher, Sandra an attorney."

"Yes. It wouldn't have been so bad if she was beautiful and dumb, but she wasn't. I ended up standing in front of children, she in front of juries. Everything she did had to be better than Rose and me."

The third morning they arrived to find Sandra unchanged, still in a coma, Dr. Carvainis and two other doctors gathered around her bed.

"Dr. Shapiro and Dr. Krige from Renal," Carvainis said.

"Is there a problem?" Erica asked.

"Do you know whether she had any alcohol that night?"

"I don't know. Is it important? I didn't see her that night." Which was true. She was at the cinema with a friend, and hadn't seen Sandra all Wednesday.

"The acid levels in her blood are abnormal. It would help us to know whether it came from alcohol or something else."

"She's also developed pneumonia," Carvainis added. "She's intubated, lying in one position, infection's one of the risks from the tubes being in the lungs for such a long time. Tomorrow should tell us more. But there's some good news. Her pupils responded to light."

"And her chances, doctor?" Rose asked. "I know it's an unfair question, but when she wakes up can you give us a little hope? What about her brain?"

Carvainis, they'd heard was a brilliant technician with the bedside manner of a toad.

"Well, she's one sick puppy, and head injuries are hard to predict. Even when she comes out, it'll be difficult to assess the long-range cognitive deficits. But it's a moderately severe injury, there was severe trauma to the brain" and half grinning, added, "There'll probably be one less lawyer now."

Shapiro and Krige looked at each other and left.

"I beg your pardon?"

"What I meant was, there're better jobs than lawyers."

"This is —"

But a nurse called him to the phone, and he took off.

Rose turned to an officious-looking woman in a black-and-red cape.

"Sister, did I hear right?"

Sister Wessels gave the weary smile of an exasperated mother who'd just been told her child had bullied someone on the school grounds again. "Don't take it to heart. Look how short he is — his foot's practically wedged in his mouth."

"We always knew, both of us, that there was something between us — a wall, distance, that we would never be close. I think I erected it and everything followed from there."

"Ordinary sibling rivalry, jealousy?"

"Can jealousy be ordinary? I hated her. On my third birthday, my mother's water broke right in the middle of cutting the cake. They took her into the bedroom where the midwife rolled up her sleeves and ordered hot water and towels, and everyone forgot about me. That afternoon, my cousins still eating the last of the cake and ice cream, my father acting like Puck in *A Midsummer Night's Dream* came out with her all wrapped in a lemon shawl, 'Look everyone, a little boer!' Knocked for a shilling by a white child. And when that fuzz turned silver and she focused those violet eyes, it was as if some honour had been bestowed on the family, some legitimacy. See my child? This is who we are. My father took her with him to the bank when he wanted a loan, and to Kenilworth Race Track when he wanted to sit in the white pavilion.

"White people are civilized, the rest a river of inarticulate ingrates. You say *yes baas* and hear *hotnot* in return. So when by some fluke a whiteskin's born to coloured folk you can't blame them if they lose sight of who they are. They've been validated. You tell someone long enough he's ugly, he believes it."

"You can certainly pass."

"'A monkey with a golden ring still remains a hairy thing.' One time on a Jo'burg flight I let an Afrikaner carry my bags to the airport lounge. It was a disgustingly good feeling because he was in his chocolate-browns. Army. Keeper of the land. He would've thrown up if he knew where I lived, that my nose had been trimmed with a knife."

"Tell us about Mr. Stone."

"Lionel Stone. Maybe I should start with Claude Brown, the student I brought home when I was sixteen to help me with math."

"There's definite improvement. This morning her hand reached up to pull the tube from her mouth, there's much more movement now. We're prodding her on the hour to try and wake her, there's been some response. Stand on the other side of the bed, Rose, and we'll see if we have any luck."

The nurse pinched Sandra on the arm, talking directly into her ear, "Sandra, wake up!"

Nothing.

She pinched harder, raising her voice. "Wake up, Sandra! You're in the hospital! Can you hear me?"

The ventilator was the only sound, raising and dropping her chest.

Erica arrived, and they went downstairs to the cafeteria.

"There's some improvement, she tried to pull the tube

out of her mouth. It means she's in there, Erica, struggling to come out. She's coming back to us."

"And she will."

Rose blew loudly into her handkerchief. "How was the funeral?"

"The coffin was closed."

"Really? Was he disfigured?"

"I don't know. No one acknowledged me."

"What did you expect? He was in her bed. And the family didn't like her very much. Isn't that what you said?"

"Something like that."

"I didn't know you knew them."

"Mmmm."

They ate their yogurt in silence.

"Erica?"

"What?"

"Did you know him before her?"

"When I turned twenty-one — don't forget, our birthdays were on the same day — my parents gave me a twenty-first at Woodstock Town Hall with caterers, a band, a sterling-silver key for unlocking my future, and all. It was a triple celebration because Sandra was also turning eighteen, and I was getting engaged that night.

After the announcement and the ring, and many dances around the floor, he left with her for a *braai* in the Glen. Just like that. She just sucked him in like a stick of Juicy Fruit, spitting him out when the flavour was gone. I was sick for a month after that."

The cigarette sizzled in the bottom of the Coke can.

"Then a friend of mine was doing a promotion on

condoms and I had a box mailed to her. After pricking holes through the cellophane. Can I have another cigarette?"

The hand flicked a Stuyvesant out of the pack.

"When she fell pregnant, I took her to this woman in Walmer Estate. My mother never found out. Not long after that, she dumped him for someone else."

"Sandra, wake up!"

Sister Wessels was bent over the bed, the ivory hand lost in her grip.

Rose had had a strange dream. Three of them at a wedding, Sandra's long hair shimmering in the morning light, laughing at the top of the steps, Erica in a black veil following pallbearers down a hill to a banjo beat. Why was her dead mother the bride and Sandra wearing the gown? And Erica still with the police?

"Wake up!" Sister Wessels barked.

A muscle twitched and Rose felt her heart skip a beat.

Sister Wessels took a firmer grip and spoke again.

"Move your thumb!"

Nothing.

"Sandra, you're in the hospital! Move your thumb if you can hear me!"

An eyelash fluttered.

The old nurse had the cold hand in both of hers. "MOVE YOUR THUMB, SANDRA! MOVE IT IF YOU CAN HEAR ME, GIRL!"

And then the index finger moved.

Sister Wessels patted the cold hand, and put it gently back under the covers.

"She's got her signals crossed, but she's there."

"The year before she graduated she brought home this new student — she was always bringing home students so no one took notice of any of them. Lionel was at U.C.T. studying archaeology, interested in the Dead Sea Scrolls and all the controversy. After they'd dated three or four months, he arrived one night to pick her up and she wasn't there. She'd made arrangements to go to the movies with him, but had run into an old flame and when he asked her out, she just took off without a thought. She was very careless that way, knew they'd always come back.

"So there I was with my hands on my grilled cheese, having nowhere to go on a Saturday night, listening to him trying to be polite about her inconsiderateness. After he'd gotten it off his chest, he left, and never called again. I liked that. And by the time she remembered or cared to remember, she was into her safari phase, and there was a conservationist.

"A year later I run into Lionel at the Piaf Revue at the Space and we go for coffee. He'd been to the Qumran Caves, graduated, and was living in a cottage in Newlands. Two days later I get a call, and it's him saying he has tickets for a new play at the Nico Malan. I can't figure it out, but say yes and we go.

"When there was a fifth and a sixth and a seventh time and we were calling each other and pressing lips at the Moonlight Grill in Claremont, I took it serious. I didn't delude myself though that he'd fallen in love — I wasn't giving hives, but wasn't stopping traffic on the street with my looks, either. I wasn't that naive. So I tiptoed in and went to the symphony, the beach, restaurants, dancing

my Saturday nights away at Bad Heart in the Trust
Tower. I'd found the right one at last. He'd not only seen
the competition, he'd had it. No danger there. Then, on
New Year's Eve he had a puncture on De Waal Drive
and was late picking me up for dinner at Constantia Nek.
Sandra opened the door when he arrived.

"I'd often wondered how it would be if the shoe was
on the other foot, but seeing her mouth drop open in
shock, I felt no victory. Looking from Lionel to me, it
sank in slowly and, almost in admiration, she laughed
and said it was great. He asked how she was keeping —
did she graduate, work? — and we left. But I knew from
the way her left dimple moved when she smiled that it
had happened again."

She took the last cigarette.

"He never mentioned her over dinner, and that said
lots. When I arrived at his cottage the next day for lunch,
her car was parked in front."

"Is that — ?"

"Yes. I sat in the car for three hours. Through the gate
I saw them head for the swimming pool. That's when I
lost it and got the idea to hire someone."

❖

THE STARLIGHTS

THE SUN CROUCHED LOW in the west, reflecting off the rooftops of District Six like red glints in a leopard's eye.

Nestled at the foot of Table Mountain, District Six looked its best during that half hour when the last amber rays brought a gentle glow to its cheeks. The heartbeat of Cape Town — here was the stink of fish and the fragrance of roses and carnations, the muezzin calling the faithful to prayer, the cries of a man being stabbed, and poignant, penny-whistle blues in the street.

Hanover Street twined its way through a maze of dilapidated buildings from Max Ginsberg's tea strainers and silk at the top of the hill to Gatiepie's live chickens and goats: a subway of wholesalers, stalls, tailors, fish-and-chips shops, *doekoems*, herbalists, hairdressers, bioscopes, pickpockets, *tjotjie* boys, and hawkers. "Pawpaws en pineapples, merem. Two for a rand, jus' for you." The odours and aromas drifting out of restaurants and salons blended with the human sweat and petrol fumes of overloaded double deckers grunting up the hill, narrow side streets jammed with small houses pocketed between top-heavy double-stories with perilous balconies closing out the sky, clouded by makeshift lines with wet sheets flapping in the breeze. Sometimes the lines hooked up with lines on the other side, and bloomers and pyjamas blew like streamers over the heads of vendors and cars on the streets.

On Sundays the Christians brightened the streets with their floral prints and psalm books; on Fridays, the Muslims with their fezzes and suits. Church bells got the same respect as the Adhaan five times a day and, during Ramadan, a lull fell over the slope.

At Noortjie's, on the corner of Hanover and Arundel, the Starlights leaned against the cement post jingling the change in their pockets, cigarettes dripping from their lips.

"Where's dat *roeker*?" Toetkuif asked. *Toet* literally meant vagina, *kuif* an Elvis Presley bouffant. He was so nicknamed because his kinky hair, heavily pomaded, was styled in a stiff point over his forehead.

"He know mos we got a job on," the poet chorused, taking out his harmonica and brushing his thick lips over the instrument, warming up.

"It's *pwasa*, man. Maybe's he's fasting," Tackies said.

"Dat *roeker* don' fast, man," Toetkuif said. "A man what drive a car in robberies eat in Ramadan."

"No, man," Tackies persisted. "'Member Gammat? He could throw a knife a hundred yards an' loosen your bag without touching your hand, but when it come to fast, man, dat *roeker*'s off de streets."

"You have a mother like Galiema Klip, you also be off de street."

"You know mos I don' have a mother, why you talking *kak*?"

"Okay, okay, don' get your *dinges* in a jam. Why dey call you tackies anyway? You don' wear no san' shoes, man."

"Taliep dem mos got a letter dis week."

"Us too."

"Everyone got one," Poet said. "De whole District Six."

"Where's you people going?"

"Bonteheuwel. If we get a council home."

"Bonties? Dat's mos jus' wind 'n dust, ou pel. It take two hours for a bus to town."

"What dey gonna do here, in District Six?"

"Bom' it down forre whites. Dose vokking boere mos wan' everyting."

"Shit!" Toetkuif spat a ball of phlegm on the pavement. "Dat *roeker* better show up, man. Three stereos, Cyril said. We need de van, rent's coming up."

"Everyone's mos buying stereos now," Poet said. "Even de ouens what eat mealie pap at night."

The police van came coasting down the hill, eight drunks crammed in the aerated hold in the back. Sergeant Wynand, his golden-haired arm out the window, ordered his young partner to bring the van to a halt. The most hated boere boy to descend on District Six, the sergeant *knobkierried* first, asking questions when he had his boot on your back in the dust.

He swung out his legs, tapping his *knobkierrie* against his fist.

"What you boys hanging around dis corner for keeping it warm?"

"Dere's mos not a law against it, sir," Poet said.

Wynand looked at the olive-skinned youth.

"Don't keep yourself a smart kaffir, hey. Pasop!"

"Hey, Poet," Toetkuif warned, throwing him a look.

"I get any complaints, I'll be after you *hotnots* faster than the *tokeloshe*."

The radio crackled, and the young constable leaned out his head. "There's a stabbing on McGregor, sir."

Wynand nodded, and went into the store, his indifference giving his young partner the shits. Dolf hated driving this beat with the sergeant, but didn't know how to ask for a transfer without insulting him.

Inside Noortjies, Mister Noor saw the blue uniform darken his door, and immediately reached behind him for a packet of Stuyvesant 25s.

"A iron brew, too. Cold."

The Indian went to the cooler and took out the drink, embarrassed at the huge Afrikaner patting his pockets for change. It wasn't creative anymore.

"That's awright, sergeant. Next time," he said, knowing full well that next time would never come.

Wynand touched his finger to his forehead in a salute, picked up what he had loafed and left.

"We have to hurry, sir," Dolf said, panicking a little.

"We'll get there, man, don't lose your sausage 'n eggs. Those hotnots can wait. Let's get rid of these drunks in the back."

"It's a stabbing, sir, the man's bleeding —"

Wynand shot him a look, and Dolf reversed the van and turned left.

Mister Noor breathed a sigh of relief. He had fasted all day, and in a few minutes the call would sound from the minaret for maghrib prayers, and his wife would bring him a plate of curried fish from the back. Fridays were big headaches in District Six with all the paypackets flying and skollies lying in wait at bus stops to relieve the unwary of their dough. He'd also had a splitting migraine all day. The Starlights seemed edgy, and he hoped there would be no trouble that night. He had long ago given up

trying to drive them off, and in the end it was them or
Boeta's Boys, a gang so fearful they knocked on doors
warning people to keep their children inside when a fight
was coming down, leaving victims with knife wounds in
the street — regularly providing the Starlights with cigarettes to keep the peace and protect his turf. A cut above
the other gangs with their harmonies, two-tone shoes,
turned-up collars and baggy pants; the Starlights also
had a code of honour and only stole from whites.

"There's de *bilal*," Toetkuif said, hearing the adhaan
from three different mosques. "Taal's not coming now."

Poet took the harmonica from his mouth, and Toetkuif
gave him the eye.

"What you stopping for, you mos not 'n *slams*? *Speel*."

"*Soema*. Respeck, man. You know, mos. Listen to dat
ou, he's making music, man."

"Here comes Merle 'n Hil'ry," Tackies edged a little
closer to the door through which the girls had to pass.

"Hil'ry's showing it, ou pel. You go for her, I'll teckle
Merle."

"No, I like Merle, you go for Hil'ry. I don' like all dat
sticky hair. Hey, Merle!" Poet called. "Come here girl.
You mos got 'n lekker pair o' pearls."

The others laughed, and Mr. Kannemeyer's sixteen-
year-old daughter threw her head back as if her kinky
bush would move off her forehead.

"Merle, girl, you wanna come with Poet for a whirl?
He'll put you in a *moena* swirl."

Merle came bravely up onto the cement, and Poet,
resplendent in his shirt with the silver armbands he'd
knuckle-dusted off a man a few weeks ago, jumped in
front of her, barring her way with his arms.

"You know mos we here every night, Merle, you an'

Hil'ry — why you come if you don' wanna *stuk*? You wanna see if Poet can *pik*?"

Merle's dress was a little revealing for a walk to the corner store, and the rouge on her cheeks turned dark.

"I came to buy bread, awright?"

"*Ouens*, Merle can talk. Show us your tongue, Merle," he said, and before Merle could do anything, he had his hand on her breast, and squeezed. "Mangoes, my broer!" But as quickly as he had cupped it, he gave a sprightly step back, bowed and waved her through. Merle fairly hopped through the door, followed by Hilary fighting off Tackies who was pinching her bum.

"You got to get yourself a goose, Poet," Tackies said. "Your kettle's boiling, pel."

"De goose I get gotta have hair, man, not dat wire with all dat brilliantine. An' don' talk about me, lookit dat stick in your pants."

"Ooh *ghottala*, dere's your mother getting off de bus."

"Kevin!"

Poet sniffed, then looked up. Four houses away, her voice carried like daggers through the air.

"Come carry dese parcels home, you bogger! What you stan'ing loafing dere on de street?!"

"You better run, ou Poet, before she give you one."

"Vok it, man," he sauntered off at a skollie's trot.

Toetkuif and Tackies laughed as his mother struck him with the carrier bag against the head, Poet jumping back to avoid the blow. Then they disappeared into the twilight, Poet carrying a sack of potatoes and grocery bags. He was back in time to catch Merle and Hilary coming up the street.

"Merley, Merley, *ek vry vir jou*, girlie." And he pouted his lips suggestively. "Okay, ouens, I'm back. Dat *rocker* not here yet?"

"No, an' it's almos' nine a clock."

A car was coming up.

"It's Neville Plaatjies. Maybe he seen Taliep."

"He don' see no one, man. His mother mos *vrek* with a German, now he thinks he's white, mos. With his Standard Eight an' his high-class English."

"Dat bogger can boogie," Toetkuif said. "See him spin on de dance floor? He goes *befock*."

"Hey, Nevvy, howzit?"

"Poet, ou pel. Hooit."

"Did you see Taliep in your travels, pel?" Toetkuif asked.

"No."

"We need him for a job."

"Don' lookit me, man."

"We not looking at you, we looking at your car. An' we see you gotta goose in it. Dat de same cherry from Elsies?"

Neville was freshly pressed, new tackies on his feet. "That's my *stuk*, yes."

"Dat's mos long for you, Nevvy. Nevvy, devvy, pudding 'n pie, *naai* de girls and make dem cry."

"They don't fucking cry, man."

"See, I tol' you," Poet said. "Since his sister lef' for Australia, Nevvy thinks he's a *laan*. *They don't fucking cry, man*, he imitated. You still a skollie, pel. Spare us a coupla rand, Mister Boilermaker. You mos got all de start."

Neville reddened.

"I'm unemployed, man. Money's scarce."

"Ja, ja, we all unemployed. You karn spare a rand for a packeta fish 'n chips?"

Neville reached into his pocket.

"A rand is all I can spare, man."

"A rand is fine, ou Nevvy. We can mos come again. When you got a job."

Neville gave him the money, and Poet took out a crumpled packet of cigarettes, offering him one.

"You get de 'viction letter yet?" Tackies asked.

"Yes."

"Where you gonna live?"

"Fairways."

"Fairways? Dere's mos no *roekers* in Fairways. For de grand people, mos. A room?"

"A servants' quarters in the yard. And you?"

"Dunno."

In the distance they heard the grunting of the old Volvo, and saw the one spotlight. Neville left.

"There's dat *roeker* coming now," Toetkuif said. "Gooi a tune, my broer."

"Doo whap, doo whah..."

Poet put the harmonica to his lips.

"... *Stella by Starlight* ..."

❖

THE DOEKOEM

I WAS ON MY KNEES in front of the kitchen dresser, unpacking jam, condensed milk, lentils, beans, removing the oil cloth, wiping the area with a soapy rag, squeezing water into an enamel basin — a job I had Friday afternoons after school, as well as polishing the brass and shining up the mirrors in the house — when there was a mouselike patter and a knock and Patty's face appeared at the kitchen door.

Patty Gonzales lived with her married sister down the street, and had taken to coming to my grandmother since that time her baby had burned with a fever and Oemie had made an instant diagnosis, going outside for the stem of a plant, inserting the crushed tip into the baby's behind. The baby went blue as he howled, seconds later a brown jet shooting from his bum.

"There!" Oemie exclaimed. "Packed fulla shit as I thought," washing her hands, donating the last squash from the pantry for the baby's supper that night.

And here was Patty again, Simon on her hip, her stomach bigger than the last time.

My grandmother had been shelling peas and drew her huge body out of the chair, wrapping her long scarf tightly about her hair, rolling the ends into coils, then weaving it in under the overlapped edges.

"Come in, Patty. Long time no see."

"Yes, Mrs. Abrahams," Patty laughed nervously. "How is Mrs. Abrahams?"

"Fine, with the Grace of God. Just the leg hurts now and then, you know, when it rains. Are you having another baby, Patty?"

Patty took the seat offered, and as soon as she sat down, spluttered like a faulty sprinkler over Simon's curly head.

I knew what was next: Sabah, go play in the other room. Sabah, go do the mirrors in the lounge. *Walls have ears, you know.*

"Go see if the postman come."

"He came this morning, Oemie."

"Well, take an iceblock and go play outside, then."

I threw the dirty water in the sink, took a raspberry iceblock from the freezer tray, and ran out before she remembered the other jobs.

But I was interested in what had brought Patty again — there was sure to be a story — so I ran out the front, and crept around the side of the house. Licking the red drops dripping down my arm onto my elbow, I sat on my heels outside the kitchen window next to the drain.

"... a terrible ting ...", Patty's voice drifted out. "I wonder if Mrs. Abrahams can perhaps help me out."

It was amazing how many people came to my grandmother for help. If it wasn't for ointment for a rotten sore, for jam and bread, bus fare, advice, it was for favours way out of line. One night my mother returned from work to find a dead man laid out in the living room on the *kateel* that had arrived from the mosque. The man,

a Muslim friend of a neighbour who said the dead man
had no relatives, had died of a stroke, and my grandmother, feeling sorry for the neighbour who said he didn't
know anything about Muslim funerals, offered to take it
on. My mother arrived to a house smelling of incense and
kifaaitkos — the traditional 'funeral food' made with mut-
ton, carrots and peas— filled with strangers who'd come
to pay their respects, my grandmother floating about in
her black robes directing the show. My mother had to
stand all night serving tea, the next day scrubbing and
spraying with Beattie to get the smell of camphor and
dead body out. Beattie could do the washing and polishing and make up beds, but Beattie wasn't allowed to
touch my Friday jobs. "We want you to do these things
yourself, so you know what to expect one day."

"I came to Mrs. Abrahams because I thought perhaps
Mrs. Abrahams know of someone I can go to."

"Go to? What kind of someone?"

Patty cleared her throat.

"What kind of someone, Patty?"

"A doekoem, Mrs. Abrahams."

"A doekoem?" I heard the shock in my grandmother's
voice. The only thing I knew about doekoems was what
I'd overheard at my aunt's house. They were people with
funny eyes and strange powers and could do great
favours if you did what they asked and stayed on their
good side. Auntie Kareema's friend who was very old,
had gone to one, and gotten married afterwards to a man
who'd walked past her at the bus stop for two years.

"I don't go to doekoems, Patty. Muslims don't believe
in such things."

"I just thought perhaps if Mrs. Abrahams know someone. Doris says —"

"What you want to go to a doekoem for? They just take your money, it don't work."

There was a short silence during which the kettle was plunked on the stove.

"Does Mrs. Abrahams remember Issy Suliman?"

"The one who did the deed, and afterwards you didn't see his dust? I remember that rotter, yes. What about him?"

"There was reasons, Mrs. Abrahams. His family would've never accepted me, being an Apostolic and all."

"You make too many excuses for that boy, Patty."

"He came back," Patty continued. "After Simon was born. We talk 'n talk an' he said he wanted us to be a family."

"Well, that's something."

"I was going to convert an' change my name an' we were gonna get married by Muslim rites by dat Imam in Athlone. He said he would burn in hell if he turned, so I had to. Muslims don' turn for Christians."

"He should've thought of hell when he had you under him. And?"

"He bought dose little books from de mosque, and I met Imam Patel. I spoke to my mother, and she said —"

"What happened, Patty?"

"Well, Mrs. Abrahams —"

"Patty, get to the point."

My grandmother's a woman of little patience — no frills 'n drills, as she calls it — and I could imagine the spit on her bottom lip.

"I got pregnant again, Mrs. Abrahams. As Mrs. Abrahams can see. When I tol' him, he never came back."

I knew what was next.

"Are you surprised, Patty?"

"A man karn do all dis with a woman an' not care, Mrs. Abrahams."

"Don't talk to me about what a man can do, Patty. When that iron's standing stiff between his legs he's not thinking of anything."

"But he love me, Mrs. Abrahams. I know."

"Love?" my grandmother laughed. "Don't be getting your head full of that tommy rot. Love's for movie stars who marry four and five times and have to call it something. Forget about love. You can't think of love with one on your lap and one coming on. The right man will come when the time's right."

"He's de father, Mrs. Abrahams," Patty cried "I don' wanna be alone."

"You know, Patty, some women love to hurt. Any feeling is better than no feeling at all. Even if it kicks them in the gut. Let old Mrs. Abrahams teach you something today. I'm not an educated woman, but there's one thing I've learned being with Mr. Abrahams forty years. You *are* alone, my girl. We arrive alone and we leave alone. No one gets into the box with us when we die. Husbands come and go, children leave. Before you can depend on a man, you must be able to depend on yourself. We all want to feel safe. Especially us women who think we can't breathe without a man next to us in bed. But safety doesn't come from a man, it comes from within. You know what I'm saying? Go to church. Think about your children, get a job. If you don't mind me saying, that boy's not going to marry you. Not because of religion, that's an excuse. But because, you see, once the snake has his head in the bush, I don't want to be cruel, Patty, but, why should it come out?"

Patty wailed like an old sea horn.

"Will Mrs. Abrahams not marry again?"

"Me? No, Patty. The pistons are old and worn out, I don't have the stomach for another man. There, have some biscuits and tea and don't waste any more tears on that Issy."

Patty left soon after with a carrier bag of greens, promising to follow Oemie's advice. I thought that the end of the matter.

Three weeks later Patty was back.

"Mrs. Abrahams, can I talk to Mrs. Abrahams for a minute?"

"Yes, Patty, come in."

"He came again last night out of de blue. Can Mrs. Abrahams see what he's doing? He's very sorry, he said. His mother was sick, dat's why he couldn't come. He wants to make tings right. Clean up his mess, he said. I don't wanna believe him, but I'm going to, Mrs. Abrahams."

"Then you've decided, what can I say. But he couldn't call to tell you she was sick?"

"He had lots of tings on his min', he said. But I came to Mrs. Abrahams, because I still have dat favour to ask. I still wanna see someone. Mrs. Abrahams know what I mean?"

"I told you Patty —"

"Before he changes his mind again."

"But if he changes his mind again, it's better for you to know now — don't you see?"

"Please, if Mrs. Abrahams can help me out just dis one time."

"How, Patty? I told you I don't —"

"Doris said Mrs. Abrahams knows someone in Retreat. Mrs. Abrahams took her Ralphie dere when he had dat curse on him and he kept getting into accidents."

She finally noticed me at the table pretending to read my school books.

"Don't listen to old people's conversations. Go and play outside."

I went to the same spot under the kitchen window, and listened in.

"... it's a long time ago since I took Doris to see that man, I don't know. And Doris shouldn't be talking of such things. If my daughter found out, there'll be *oorlag* in this house."

"Please, Mrs. Abrahams. I can get a car to take us. We don' have to be long."

My grandmother was notorious for bothering neighbours for lifts, and I thought it smart of Patty to bring up the availability of a car.

"Let me think about it. It'll have to be Monday or Tuesday, during the day. I don't believe in these things, Patty, you can't mess with the Will of God. But if we go, the man charges ten rand. Bring twelve just in case. I don't think it'll work. One can't believe in God and these things at the same time. What kind of a believer will that make me? People can't perform miracles."

On Monday, when I returned from school, Oemie was wearing her black cloak over a beige dress, a cream veil, her eyes darkened with kohl. This was her only vanity, and a handsome woman my grandmother was with her skin the colour of a copper penny, her medorah flecked with gold. When you saw the kohl and smelled the eau de cologne, you knew you were going somewhere.

A peanut-butter sandwich waited for me on the kitchen table, and I hardly had time to take off my *gym* when the hooter of the car sounded outside.

"Come, come," she rushed me out the door. "We have to be back by five." And shouting back at Beattie who was seeing us off, "That meat's almost soft, Beattie. Put the potatoes in and turn the stove off in half an hour."

Beattie was good at a lot of things, but once she started listening to those afternoon serials, her brain switched off. My grandmother was taking a helluva chance with my mother's supper that night.

The car took us through side streets and avenues all the way past the Race Track, up the main road, down more streets until, twenty minutes later, we arrived in a grey little strip lined with council homes. Snot-nosed piccaninnies without underwear played in the street, unafraid of oncoming cars, dogs shitting right next to the older children playing transistor radios on the pavement.

"Did you bring something that belongs to him?" my grandmother asked.

"Yes."

"And don't look in the man's eye."

"What's wrong with his eye?"

"He's blind, I think, but I'm not sure. Don't look just in case he can see."

The driver stopped at a house with a sad-looking flower in a jam tin in the window, a beat-up Renault on cement blocks right on the small patch of sand supposed to be the front lawn.

"You better come in with us."

Did she think I was going to sit in the car?

The ground was wet from the rain and my school

walkers squished in the mud. An old woman asked us in, pointing to a dimly lit kitchen at the back.

The house was damp, with the odours of an animal barn, and I automatically dipped my nose behind my shirt collar, trying not to breathe. The curtains were drawn, even in the tiny living room we passed through where another lady sat mending clothes in the half dark, and I felt suddenly hot and tight like the time at the Cango Caves with Granpa Doels when I had crawled into a small space and for an instant was paralyzed, imagining the mountain collapsing, pushing me into the ground.

In the kitchen a dirty bulb hung from the ceiling over a red, metal-edged formica table, four chairs squeezed into the small space where two heavily made-up ladies in pressed blouses and skirts, probably customers, looked very out of place. Even more out of place was the scraggly goat not three feet from their buckled brogues, the rope around his neck hooked to the nail in the back door. The air reeked of boiled tripe and wet goat.

There was nowhere to sit, and I leaned against the back of my grandmother's chair, not knowing where to let my eyes fall. They strayed briefly to the cracked lino on the floor, the primus stove and cool-drink crate under the table, resting finally on the goat eyeing me warily from under two nasty horns. I had an uncontrollable urge to get through the door.

"Oemie? I have to pee."

"Didn't I tell you to pee before you go out."

"I forgot."

"Go ask the old lady in the front where the lavvy is."

"I'll come with you," Patty said.

"People off de street have de nerve to use it," the old

woman said, "so it's a little blocked. Dere's newspaper under a stone by de door."

The smell hit me when we rounded the house, and I despaired when I saw the wooden contraption with the hanging door, big puddles out in front.

"I can't go in, Patty. It stinks."

Patty was anxious to get back in the house.

"Dere's no one around. Why don' I stan' here, an' you pee behind de lavvy."

There was no sign of paper under a stone, and what was flying about in the yard was wet and soiled.

"Do you have any tissue?"

Patty looked in her bag. "No. Just pee, and shake it off."

The thought of squatting out in the open, in front of a stranger, the cold wind hitting my behind, made me wish Patty had kept her problems to herself. But I felt the first drops squeeze out. Squatting quickly behind the lavatory, the pee hit my shoe.

"I need some paper, Patty."

Patty looked in her bag again, and still couldn't come up with anything. Then she lifted up her skirt, and tore off a piece of petticoat.

I took the nylon square, spit on it, then wiped myself, washing my hands at the tap, dabbing cold water on my contaminated foot.

"We're next," my grandmother said when we returned to find the fancy ladies gone. "Wait here in the kitchen, we won't be long."

Me stay alone with the goat? After following the whole story?

"I don't want to sit here by myself, Oemie."

"What you scared of? That goat won't do anything.

Well come on, then."

The old lady showed us into the bedroom and closed the door. If I thought the house scary, the dwarf on the pink wicker bedspread in the hole of a room with its magazine cut-out of a sad Jesus Christ on a green wall and a half-revealed pee pot under the bed, struck new fear in my heart. Dark, with wiry hair, the doekoem was crippled and deformed, white cataracts on his eyes. His head moved when we came in, nostrils twitching as he sniffed at the air.

"*En wie kom hier?*"

"Mrs. Abrahams. Van Steurhof."

He thought for a moment. "Oo, Mrs. Abrahams. *Die kind met die krippel been.*"

"*Daai's reg. Mr. Poggenpoel het 'n goeie memory.*"

"What bring you today, missies?"

"I got someone with me."

"I know."

"She's got a problem with a man."

The old man waited.

"Patty?" my grandmother prodded. "Speak up."

Patty seemed mesmerized, but launched into a long speech, dabbing occasionally at the spit in the corner of her mouth. When she was done, ending with a long sigh, she waited for the miracle.

"Better to leave some tings," the doekoem said without turning his head. "If Mrs. Abrahams unnerstan'."

"I told her, but you know how these young people are."

"Did you bring a piece of his clothes?"

"I got one of his ties," Patty said, bringing it out of her bag.

The doekoem took it from her and threw it on the cold

cement floor between the two single beds where we sat. Then he took a stick as gnarled as himself and poked it into the maroon material, stirring it around on the floor like a witch stirring a pot of soup. I'd seen the movie with Moses, and expected to see the tie wriggle and raise its head.

"I see him coming."

"What do you mean?" Patty asked.

"I see him coming over."

How could he see Issy when he couldn't see us?

The stirring continued. "But he needs work."

"You see him coming to me?"

"Yes. But —"

"What?"

"Ssshh. Let the man do his work," my grandmother said.

For a woman who said she didn't believe in such things, she was very curious about Mr. Poggenpoel's findings on the dirt floor.

"I want to know de problem, Mrs. Abrahams," Patty said. "Maybe if I know the problem, I can fix it."

The stirring stopped, and just when I thought the doekoem had fallen asleep and forgotten us, he spoke.

"Dere's a woman."

"A woman? It karn be."

"With long hair."

We waited.

"Can Mr. Poggenpoel help me den?" Patty was desperate. Her hair was *kroes* as steelwool; she stood a monkey's chance.

"I can give you someting for him. It will bring him over to you."

"Really? What?"

"Some water."

"Water?"

"Special water. When you get home, fin' a bottle to put it in. Make it look like a presen' an' give it to him. Is important nothing happen to de bottle. Dat bottle stay with him seven days, he's yours."

"Can I put de water in his tea? Just to make sure?"

"De water's from a dassie's pee. If you drink it, it do someting else."

"What if de bottle breaks —"

"It mustn't."

"Or gets lost?"

The doekoem got up to indicate the visit was over.

We left there at five-thirty with water in a fish paste jar, Oemie panicking at the late hour.

"Don't let me hear you repeat any of this," she said, handing me a pink star, a candy not to tell my mother where we'd been.

We didn't see Patty again until the summertime, and then it was at the ticket counter at Steurhof station where Patty had just gotten off the train we had to take into town. Simon had grown, and was holding onto her dress, the new baby in Patty's arms.

"Patty, I haven't seen you in months. Where've you been?"

"I got me a job as a machinist in Salt River," Patty said. "Four days a week. My sister looks after dem while I work."

"And Issy."

Patty's voice made a funny sound.

"Agh, Mrs. Abrahams."

My grandmother waited.

"Mrs. Abrahams was ma right."

"What do you mean?"

"It didn't work."

"What happened?"

"De cashier at Easy-Kleen, Mrs. Abrahams. He didn't even wait for de child to be born. He got right in bed with dat Indian bitch."

"What do you mean?"

"Dat night when I gave him de bottle as de doekoem said, he put it in his jacket pocket. We had supper at a takeout in Rylands an' some curry fell on de lapel. De next day he took de jacket to de cleaners and de bottle was still in it."

"Oh, my word."

"De cashier, Mr. Abassie's daughter, Mrs. Abrahams know de one with de long, greasy plait? — she served him, and from dat day on, Mrs. Abrahams, I dunno what got into him, but he never came back."

The tale was long and sad, my grandmother forgetting all about the man waiting for us in Wynberg. We missed two trains, and ended up walking back home with Patty carrying her bags.

❖

THE BET

WE WERE ENJOYING our first open-air lunch of the season on one of those overbright days of spring when Errol spotted Sabah under a nearby umbrella.

"Isn't that that new secretary in your office, Jill? What a looker, eh?"

"She's not white, you know," Allan said.

"What do you mean she's not white. Of course she's white. Look at that hair, straighter than mine, her skin's like ivory."

"She's a convincing whiteskin," Allan said.

"Then why's she in a white restaurant?"

"Oh, please. She's a play-white, I'm telling you."

"Allan's right," I said.

"How do you know?"

"I work with her. She doesn't let on, but I know. She travels first class in the mornings. We come in on the same train."

"Then maybe she really is white," Errol said.

"She isn't. There's that guttural thing that comes out."

"She's emigrating to Canada," I threw in. "A lot of them are leaving."

"That doesn't mean anything. Whites are going, too. To the U.K., Australia, everywhere."

"Not in the same numbers. Besides, I just know from the way she acts, and the things she doesn't talk about."

"Perhaps you're right," Errol grinned. "Pity. Allan's still looking for a date for New Year's Eve. Say, I have a great idea."

"I don't like it when you have that look on your face."

"You don't have the guts, never mind."

"What's this idea, for God's sake?"

"Ask her out."

"On a date you mean?"

"After the date, you have to take her home, right?"

"Right."

"If she's a play-white, we'll catch her out by her coloured address."

"That's a bit cold, don't you think?"

"Free drinks at the Rotunda if you take it on."

"How many rounds?"

"As many as you want."

"What do you think, Jill?"

"Leave me out of this. I work with her."

"But we'll need your ideas."

Sabah Solomon was the new legal secretary for Miller, Strauss where I was an articling student. She had come to Errol and Allan's attention when they picked me up at the office one day. All in our final year, Errol and Allan were articling at Abercrombie's, and we often went together to university on Wednesday afternoons.

I knew her a little, I said, as much as one can get to know someone in four months, but had no idea of her personal life. We'd sort of become friends, doing the cryptic crossword together on the train. Trying to work out a nine-letter anagram, I told her about Errol, how we almost broke up over Sally Corrigan. I was surprised, telling someone I hardly knew, especially someone like her, but she was easy to talk to, and actually had a few good opinions. Still, she was mighty silent about her personal life. A better dresser than me — coloured girls knew a lot about fashion and little about the real world — I was curious.

"She lives somewhere in Rondebosch East, someone said."

"Where in Rondebosch East? There're many grey areas in there."

"What if she likes me?" Allan was suddenly concerned. "Did anyone think of that? I mean we've had a boring winter and all that, but I don't want the girl to fall in love and start hounding me."

"Think about if she doesn't, you big head, how you'll kill yourself," Errol laughed. "Besides, she's not going to cancel her trip to Canada for you, old boy."

"We'll come with you if you like," I offered.

"But what will we talk about? We have nothing in common."

"She's not stupid, Allan. She goes to the movies, the theatre, the rugby game. We'll all be there. Just don't ask her awkward things."

"Does she dance?"

"Of course she does. They're the best dancers, you know. Haven't you seen the coon carnival?"

"That's gross."

We all laughed.

"So, what do you say? Are we on?"

"She only knows me from seeing me with the two of you."

"We'll do lunch, all of us," I said. "I can arrange it. Then ask her out."

"This is all so contrived."

"Think of the Rott. You still owe me for the last time. This will square things up."

Allan leaned back and let the sun warm his face and neck. Allan was Jewish, didn't have Errol's blue eyes and platinum looks, but was good-looking in a dark sort of way, and very popular with the girls. Ever since his break-up with Judith Asherson, he was a hit-and-run catastrophe.

"All right, then. You're on."

And so we set about the seduction of Sabah.

We decided Errol would have a birthday to give me an excuse to plan a surprise lunch — was she interested in contributing to a small gift and coming along to celebrate at the Savoy? I knew she would come once she'd contributed, and knew she wouldn't not contribute.

She wore the pale blue suit she'd bought at Truworths, and with her long brown hair shimmering, eyes sparkling, we all had second thoughts. She was light-hearted and fun, unsuspecting, and didn't appear at all uncomfortable, showing a talkative side.

"I'm having a gin and tonic for starters," I said.

"We have to go back to work after, don't forget," she reminded.

Was that a yes or a no? And then she shocked the hell out of the three of us.

"I have some really good stuff in my bag, though."

"Stuff?"

"Yes," she said, looking at the menu and not at any of us. "I got it last night from a friend. Oh, don't look so shocked. It's only a packet of Marlboros. You know, those strong American cigarettes."

"I didn't know you smoked."

"I don't. Only something that gives me a buzz."

"I see," Allan said. "What else do you do for a buzz?"

"Oh, many things."

"I bet," Errol said.

I kicked him under the table.

"Like what?" he persisted.

She pushed the menu back, and looked up. "Is this all about me? I thought it was your birthday, Errol. Happy birthday. Can I ask how old?"

Caught off guard, he stammered, twenty-three.

"Here's to you, then," she said, tearing the seal off the packet, popping a cigarette between her lips. I saw one of those bad smiles on Allan's face.

We ordered roast beef and mash, she asked for fish, and I wondered if maybe she was even a Moslem, never mind a non-white. I'd not thought of that. The name. Some of them had real ringdingers. What the hell did Sabah mean? And the way it was pronounced — she'd set you straight if you said it wrong: Saa baa. Like Saha for Sahara, she'd say.

She had two cigarettes before the food arrived, Errol and Allan helping out, stinking up the air, another after dessert. Sabah and Allan actually hit it off, and Errol and I waited patiently for him to make a move. I think Sabah even suspected something was supposed to happen. But the bill came, and Allan just sat there like a puffbird, a little fogged from the smokes and Sabah's unexpected wholesomeness.

Two days later, Mildred, the tea girl, came to Sabah's desk where I was stapling documents for Registry Office.

"A parcel for Miss Solomon."

Sabah opened it skeptically in front of Margaret and Pearl, who had stopped typing to see what it was.

"Oh, my word."

"What is it?"

"It's a wood carving. Is this black ivory?"

"It's beautiful," Margaret said. "Who's it from?"

Sabah searched around in the box.

"There's no card with it."

She looked at me. I was sure from the heat in my cheeks that my face had gone red.

"It's lovely," I said.

"But who —"

"Call for you, Sabah," Pearl called from her desk.

I heard the catch in her voice. "Who?" she said into the mouthpiece, looking at me. Then the caller hung up.

"Miss Solomon's life is very exciting," Mildred said, sorting the post. "Las' month a visa for Canada, now a secret admirer. Miss Solomon is lucky."

"Stop calling me Miss Solomon, Mildred. And I told you I've changed my mind. I'm not going to Canada."

"I'm glad, 'cause we'll miss Miss Solomon. Right, Pearl? We didn't like dat other girl from Salt River, sending me an' Naidoo all over for things."

They were fond of her, the tea girl and messenger, Mildred making special sandwiches when Sabah forgot her lunch or didn't want anything from the cafe, Naidoo regularly picking up her cashew nuts on Fridays at Wellington Fruits. But not leaving for Canada? This was news.

In my office, I called Allan.

"Was it you who sent the gift?"

"Yes."

"Why anonymously?"

"I thought I would work her up. Make it more exciting. Mysterious."

"But an African woman with a child? What were you thinking?"

"I didn't know what to send."

"What happened to roses or a nice box of chocolates?"

"Boring."

"I just heard she's not going to Canada."

"Really? Maybe we should call it off. What if —"

"Oh, stop it, you fool. You're not interested, are you?"

"Of course not."

"So, there."

The next day a single rose arrived. With a note.

"It's from Allan," she blushed. "He wants to take me out."

"Really?" I had expected more enthusiasm. "That's great. Are you going to go?"

"I don't know."

"You don't know?" How could she refuse someone like Allan? She should've felt flattered. What kind of men did she date that she was confused?

"Why would he be interested in me?"

"Why not? Don't you like him, then?"

"Who wouldn't like someone like him? It just doesn't feel right."

A horrible sensation went through me.

"What do you mean?"

"I don't know. I mean I had a good time at lunch, he's a lot of fun, but I usually know when someone likes me back. That's why I smoked so much. I was nervous he might pick up I liked him."

"So you *do* like him?"

"Yes."

"Well, that's why people go out on dates, Sabah. If you like him, and he's asked you out, I don't see the problem. I tell you what. We'll all go together, the four of us. To make it easier."

She still seemed unconvinced.

"It's not a proposal, Sabah. Just a date."

The next morning she announced she was making an appointment to cut off her hair — the Twiggy look was very much the rage — and she was buying a black mini outfit for her date.

"So you're going, then?"

"It's only a date, as you say. What do I have to lose?"

I felt like such a dog.

The night of the date we met her in front of Scarlett's Run. She was spending the afternoon in Sea Point, she said, it would be easier for her friends to drop her off there than for us to pick her up. Smart move, I thought, but there's still the ride home.

We arrived ten minutes late and found her knocking her knees, shivering in the cold breeze whipping off the ocean, looking like a waif in her Carnaby dress, Twiggy lashes, and boyish haircut. The transformation was so complete, so white, I felt sick.

We started off with drinks, then hopped in the car for supper and dancing at Felix the Cat. When they didn't come back from the dance floor for three songs, Errol and I looked at each other, considering that we might possibly have started something. We were all on the balcony watching the moon's silver runners on the dark surf, breathing in the freshness of the sea, when Sabah went to talk to the pianist. Must be requesting a tune. The pianist conferred with his band, and we choked on our drinks when we saw her walk to the centre of the stage, take the microphone, and belt out Miriam Makeba's "Click Song."

"You never said she sang."

"I didn't know." I was flabbergasted.

"A bloody decent voice, too. Good God, is there anything else we don't know?"

"I don't think so, but tell me, Allan, what happens next week?"

"What do you mean?"

"I mean, what will you do about Sabah?"

"Nothing. One goes on a date and things don't work out. Happens all the time."

"I can't go through with this."

"It's a little late to get holy on us now. It was your idea."

"My idea? It was Errol's. What if she likes you?"

"That's what I asked you, remember? She doesn't, does she?"

"She does."

"Oh, shit!"

Our conversation was interrupted by the applause, and Sabah walking back towards us.

"I didn't know you sang, Sabah," I said, genuinely surprised. "That was great."

"Thank you," she laughed, the colour back in her face. "I have a permanent arrangement on Friday nights in a club."

"I'd better not ask what else you do for fun," Errol laughed. "And all this on Seven-Up."

"I did have a little something before I came."

"Marlboros?"

"A real *skuif*."

Skuif! Not that we all didn't do dagga — *skuif* just wasn't in our vocabulary. Had she let it slip purposely?

"No!" Allan teased, "A nice girl like you?"

"Yes," she laughed, lapping it up like an eager puppy, showcasing her talent, her derringdo. Making herself irresistible.

"What time is it?" she asked when the waiter came for a last order of drinks.

"Three."

"Three? Oh, my word."

"We should get going," Allan said.

The wind was much stronger now, flapping our dresses and jackets about our heads, and we were happy to get into the warm comfort of Errol's car.

"Who's first?"

"Sabah?" I said. She sat next to Allan in the back, a little in the doldrums.

"Are you all right?"

"I didn't know it was so late."

"Are your parents waiting up then?"

"No. They're not expecting me. I was going back to my friends in Sea Point. But it's too late to knock on their door now, I'll have to go home."

I couldn't bear the look on her face.

"Do you want to come home with me?" Bet or no bet, I couldn't go through with it. "In the morning I can take you home or call a cab."

For a moment I thought she would grab at the idea of the cab.

"No. It's better for me to go home."

"Where to then?" Errol asked.

"Do you know Rondebosch East at all?"

"A little, yes. You can show me the way."

And so we sat in the car, listening to the Dave Clark Five on the radio, although I felt sure Errol and Allan's hearts were ticking as fast as mine. The bastard bet we'd made. Maybe I'd been wrong, and she really was one of us. Wouldn't that be a panic? There were Lebanese and Egyptians living in South Africa now, given white privileges — I'd already made her Moslem because of the name — maybe she was one of them. Allan talked about his upcoming cricket match, letting her know that his life didn't include females all the time, and I didn't dare look at Sabah. We were in Rondebosch East now, still in the white part, when suddenly she said, "You can stop here. At the bridge coming up."

The steep bridge over the train station was the crossover point. On this side a grey area, the other side the sprawling coloured population of Athlone. More crimes were committed in Athlone than anywhere else in the Cape.

"Here?" Errol asked incredulously, reluctant to stop the car. There was only a bus stop at the foot of the bridge, a handful of houses half a mile away.

"It's just a short walk from here."

"Let me drive you home, then. This looks so isolated."

"I don't want my parents waking up. Don't worry, it's all right."

She got out, in the middle of nowhere, and we watched as she crossed to go under the bridge. She hadn't brought a cardigan, and the wind whipped her mini around her waist, exposing her thin thighs and white underwear.

"Anyone can be lurking under that bridge." I felt suddenly scared. "Why the hell did we do this?"

"That's not where she lives," Allan said. "Wait."

We drove a little way off, then stopped the car behind a municipal building, hidden from sight.

"There. She's coming back. Going over the bridge. What did I tell you? A play-white! Get your wallet ready, old boy."

I COUNT THE
BULLETS SOMETIMES

I RECKON BEFORE I TELL YOU about Jeremy Vosloo, I should start with two years ago, the year the blacks started protesting the use of Afrikaans in their schools in Soweto and the protests grew into riots, setting off a wave of demonstrations spreading throughout the country until it arrived ugly and angry in Cape Town and my father had this bright idea to send me to private school. He always had these bright ideas, my father, from the brooders and turkey-cocks he brought home one Saturday afternoon in the back of the *bakkie* declaring that we no longer had to buy eggs from Mr. Doep, the chicken pen eventually growing into a cacophony of red-combed birds snapping at your heels, no one collecting the eggs or raking up, to the sheep and goats, and a stubborn ewe charging all the visitors. My father, you see, had grown up one of nine sons in a box in District Six, and had dreamed of a backyard where he could swing his arms without knocking into his neighbour's lavatory. When his clothing factory landed this big account, taking fashion stores from Cape Town to Mafeking, we moved from comfortable quarters on the slopes of Walmer Estate, where there was life and civilization, to this remote place in Philippi he likes to call the farm. Now, despite all the sudden complaints after the lorry pulled away with our things — the place had been too cramped, too high on the hill, the hot-water cylinder didn't hold enough — there was something about that Ravenscraig Road beauty, all highly polished oak smelling of lavendar wax and my grandmother's *tamaletjies*, crunchy squares made with pine nuts and brown sugar, warm and sticky when poured into paper moulds, that was hard to resist. The kind of house you could run through from front door to kitchen and out the back in four seconds flat and travel years with all the history and life steeped in those high beams and plastered walls. And that's another thing. Even my illiterate grandmother sitting with her huge bum on our folded pyjamas, pressing them on the stoep, eating raspberry iceblocks with condensed milk with Sies Galima from across the street, needed some kind of excitement to survive, and refused to come with us, moving in with my uncle down the street. In any event, my father bought this plot, called in contractors and landscape artists and, with the blessings of Barclays Bank, produced for his family a Cape Dutch-style home, oak doors with curved fanlights and brass knobs, velvet lawns, stables, servants' quarters, a pool, and a pack of trained Dobermans. The fantasy was started and all sorts of animals arrived. The problem was, the more animals came, the more people were hired, my father worked harder, not getting to enjoy the smell of all this warm chicken shit. So when he pushed his *Argus* aside one night, looking at my mother who was the real floor director, and broke the news that I was starting at a boys' high school in Bishopscourt, I wondered if he'd gone mad. My cousin Rudwan already said we lived like we thought we'd been born in the saddle when not one of us had raised a leg over the fillies in the yard, and here he was setting me farther apart. Private school, I argued, was for those coloureds salivating through plate glass windows at the world of the whites. Didn't I already read the news in the *Argus* every night? Wasn't my English better than my sisters, who still got it wrong translating literally from Afrikaans?

But I really should start with that first day, my mother driving me in the silver Benz, depositing me new satchel and all in front of this school with hundreds of green-blazered boys on the grounds, the only *snoek* in a sea of yellowtail. I knew I was in the right class when I saw my name on the board, and in the wrong school when I stood by myself during break. I cursed my parents. How could they do this to me when I could've been a shot with Rudwan at Sinton High? Then I noticed this boy with platinum hair and a cowlick, a garden snake in his hand, chasing after a fat student called Albert Mostert — imagine an atrocity like Albert— who was clearly horrified. Albert's short legs carried him chop chop to the principal's office where Jeremy got a warning, quickly relieved of his pet. Sitting three seats behind them in Biology, I watched Jeremy look furtively behind him, take a chameleon out of his pocket, and put it down Albert's neck. Albert jumped up with a scream, Mr. Greaves dropped the chalk, demanding the name of the culprit. Jeremy looked about, curious as the rest of the class to see who had done the deed. It looked like I'd found a friend.

That weekend Rudwan visited, and watched from the safe side of the henhouse while I waded through a gang of angry birds collecting eggs for a neighbour, my *takkies* crunching in the grey and white shit. I mean, were we an eggerama or something? We ate so many things made with eggs — puddings, omelettes, souffles — you could pull fat worms from our veins. The pittance charged didn't even cover the chicken feed.

"I'm on the swimming team."

"There's a pool?"

"And a tennis court and pingpong room."

He hung his head, and the zing went out of the brag. "But they're too strict, you can't even chew gum on the school grounds."

"What?"

"And don't let them catch you wearing your uniform after school on the street. They also have this stupid rule that if a teacher comes down the stairs, you have to stop and let him pass, and say, good morning, sir, or afternoon, sir, and not move until he does."

"That's stupid. Sinton hasn't got sturvy rules like that, and you can eat and chew what you want. Did you make any friends?"

"Yes."

"Who?"

"Jeremy Vosloo."

"Sounds like a boer."

"He is. You want to go catch tadpoles after I take in the eggs?"

We went out with our jars, but it wasn't the same as before. At supper my sisters, taking advantage of Rudwan's presence and my father's good mood, put forth their case.

"I don't see why he gets to go to private school when we have to go around here," Layla, my youngest sister complained. "He gets everything."

"Shut up, Layla. You're only in Standard Two."

"I won't shut up. You get so much things just 'cause you're a boy."

"So many things."

"Stop correcting everyone. And keep quiet both of you," my mother warned.

"Layla's right. I'm going to high school next year. Will it be private school, too?" Soraya asked.

"We'll see your marks in June."

My father waited for his youngest child, but Ruby was far too busy with her food, sucking on the bone of her chop. Ruby didn't care if she ever saw a classroom. All the notes and phone calls that came from the teachers were about Ruby. Ruby didn't do her homework, Ruby came to school with one shoe, Ruby came without a consent form for the outing to the museum, Ruby's failed math for the fourth time, Ruby's drawings won first prize.

"And you, Ruby? You want to go to private school too?"

Ruby licked her fingers, "I told you, I'm going to be an artist."

"And what kind of money do you think you'll earn?"

"I don't know. But you said we could choose."

"You want to sell paintings in Greenmarket Square and starve?"

"I'll be married, daddy. My husband will take care of the money part."

My father put his fork down, and laughed. When Ruby was three and refused to wear anything but purple underwear, he sent his typist to Woolworths for two dozen in that shade. I had to wait six weeks for Pacman, and Ruby had only to pout and flash those almond eyes and my father would nod his okay.

After I'd been at my new school three months, I asked if I could have Jeremy over for the weekend. My mother said yes, but my father couldn't quite wrap himself around the idea of an Afrikaner boy in his home. Family visited on weekends, he said, he didn't want trouble and envy surrounding his son. But he agreed, with conditions and warnings.

The factory closed at four on Fridays, the one day we could count on him to sit down to supper with us, and a favourite time because he would listen to grievances, hand out pocket money, toffee rolls, comic books, putting Milano's troubles behind him for a few hours. I must say I was most anxious to see what he thought of my blue-eyed friend — also nervous about my sisters putting me in the eyes. In between helpings of mash and peas, I found him glancing occasionally at Jeremy; how he held the fork, cut his meat, the way he put the food in his mouth — not too different from us except eating a little slower, giving a few more chews. But then Jeremy didn't have three siblings rushing to prong their forks into the last chop. Jeremy had a good way of speaking to his elders, sort of well-behaved without being overly reserved, and my father was impressed by things like that. Of course he had no idea that Jeremy was Mr. Greaves' worst nightmare.

"What're your plans for the future, Jeremy, do you know what you want to be?" I suddenly heard him ask.

"Yes, sir, I want to be a pilot."

"You don't have to call me sir, Mr. Levy's fine. A pilot?

That's nice. You like planes then, do you?"

"My father was a fighter pilot."

"Really?"

"He was killed in an air raid five years ago."

Something went the wrong way down my father's throat, and he coughed.

"I'm sorry."

"That's all right, Mr. Levy. You didn't know."

"My mom's a designer," Layla said. "She makes all the patterns for my father's factory. And yours?"

"A police sergeant."

"A woman police sergeant? Does she come home with a gun?" Ruby asked.

"Don't be stupid, silly. Sergeants don't carry guns."

"She has one, yes. I count the bullets sometimes."

A sergeant? Fighter pilot? Protecting South Africa's inhabitants? His father dying for the country? Who couldn't hold onto that?

The next morning my father was ready to drive off in his *bakkie* when Ruby ran out to say Rudwan was on the phone. My father had his key in the ignition, but leaned out the window, eyes punctuating every comma and full stop. "He's your cousin, be nice." He had this stupid fear that because I was friends with Jeremy, I was going to think I was white. Parents, I tell you. They put you out in this dinghy without a life jacket, then blame you if you drown.

Rudwan arrived in the middle of our gluing together a complicated windmill made out of sucker sticks, and I knew the minute he pretended Jeremy wasn't in the room that inviting him had been a mistake.

"Let's play *kennetjie*," he suggested. He was a whiz at hitting the stubby stick over the roof.

"It's getting dark, and we have to glue everything together tonight. We can't right now."

"You can help us," Jeremy offered.

Rudwan didn't turn his head to acknowledge his presence.

"You forgot how to play *kennetjie*, now?" he persisted.

"Did I say that? I said it was getting dark. How can we see how to play? And we have to finish this."

"Let's do it later," Jeremy suggested, trying to help.

"No. Tomorrow it has to be dry."

Rudwan left mumbling, and moments later my father summoned me into the living room.

"What's going on?"

"He's being stupid."

"Now he's calling me stupid," Rudwan whined, "He's *oorgetreek* with his friend."

"I'm not *oorgetrek*, you idiot. We have to finish gluing tonight so we can paint it in the morning, and he doesn't understand. He wants to go play *kennetjie* in the dark."

"You two always get along, why're you acting this way?"

"He's forgetting who he is."

It was just the sort of thing to set my father off. I wanted to punch the sneer off Rudwan's face.

"Then why did I ask you to come, huh? And what's the big deal, anyway? We can play tomorrow, and you can brag!"

"That's it," Rudwan snorted. "I'm calling my father to pick me up."

"Stop this nonsense now," my father raised his voice. "You're not calling anyone and, you, mister, I told you beforehand what's what."

"You satisfied now, you snot? We asked if you wanted

to help, but you didn't want to. What's your problem, man?"

"Who cares about your stupid project anyway."

"That's enough!" my father roared. "Go sort your-selves out, or I'm driving everyone home!"

We slunk back into my room, and I cursed myself for inviting him that morning on the telephone. Jeremy pre-tended nothing was wrong — he'd heard everything, of course — and I felt shitty having him there. We were showing a very bad side. Worse, when I'd told Rudwan he could come, I'd not thought of the sleeping arrange-ments. To prevent war, I threw three cushions between the twin beds and tossed restlessly all night listening to their muted machine-gun farts.

The next morning, on my way to the bathroom, I over-heard my parents, who were up early for *koeksisters* and coffee.

"... on his best behaviour."

"So're we."

"You think he's sincere?"

"What do you mean?"

"You can't change what's in their hearts."

"He's a child, man. Don't look so on everything."

"But conditioned from the time he saw his black nanny staring down at him."

"It's not his fault. And it's today's children who're going to change things, not us."

"Today's black children, coloured children. Not them. You think after three centuries, they can flush it out with epsom salts? It'll take truckloads to crack all that shit."

"You must stop all this politics in front of the kids. Nazeem's already too involved."

"He *should* be aware."

"What, every kid in South Africa isn't aware?"

"You know, I like him. When he said his father had died in an air raid it brought home to me the differences between us. There *is* glory picking up the gun for your land."

1977 had started with black schools reopening amid continued student boycotts, ending with Rhodesia announcing its acceptance of one man, one vote, and Black-majority rule — a dream held by most but not all of us. Soraya came third with eighty percent, Layla passed, Ruby played the lead in *The Frog Prince*, I finished a good first year, and my mother stunned us with the announcement that the Philippi air had thrown her cycle out, and a baby was on the way.

The factory closed for the Christmas holidays, and my father made plans for a trip to the Wilderness. A few days into the arrangements I asked if I could bring Jeremy with.

"You know, Nazeem," he started, that resigned thing in his voice, "I like Jeremy, but he's come here all year now — how many times, eight, nine? — and he's never asked you to his house."

"Maybe he has a reason."

"Of course he has."

"He's not like that, daddy, you don't know him. And we can't blame him for the government."

"But what about you? Doesn't it hurt that he hasn't asked?"

"It does, when I think about it. I don't know where he lives, and he knows where we keep the cheese in the fridge. But we're friends, and he's going nowhere for the holidays."

"His family's never tried to find out about us. You don't think we'd let you spend weekends at someone's house without knowing who they were? This is two weeks in the Wilderness."

"His mother's a sergeant, maybe she checked us out."

That night at supper he discussed it with my mother.

"Bring him with," she said.

"I don't know why I bother to ask you. You'll bring the whole Zulu tribe if you can. You have four children, you know, not yet five. Don't you find it strange that his mother's never called us?"

"Yes, but if that's how they do things and he wants to come, why not?"

My father gave in, and the day before the trip my mother and I went to pick Jeremy up. I don't know what I expected at 63 Crosby Street, but the fantasy died a cruel death when we stopped in front of this crumbly-walled cottage with an overgrown path, a rusted bicycle leaning against a wheelbarrow growing weeds under a mulberry tree with trampled berries on the hard ground. I wanted to believe we were at the wrong house, make things fit in my head, when the front door opened and Jeremy, who must've been watching from the window, came out with his rucksack and fishing rod. No one saw him off.

He got in, and we all sat heavy with our thoughts. When we arrived at the wrought-iron gates to Faan and the gardeners, the Dobermans jumping the car, our spirits lifted, and I was even glad to see my sisters, dying to show off the trailer my father had rented.

Later that evening Jeremy and I packed the coolers with frozen chops, and *boerewors*, afterwards stealing smokes from the head gardener in the backyard. One of our favourite things was sitting with Faan and Piet outside their quarters dragging on their hand-rolled cigarettes, talking nonsense; but that night Jeremy was strangely reserved. I don't know if it was the tobacco, the trip, the stop at his house, but several times while *kafoefieing* with the boys, I caught him staring off in the dark.

At eleven my mother turned off the TV, and we went to bed. Shortly after midnight, somewhere in the dimness of sleep, I heard the gates roll open, the car in the garage, then a familiar voice. I perked my ears, and turned to Jeremy in the next bed. He wasn't there. Through the window I saw his white hair reflected in the moonlight, standing on the verandah in the dark.

"... I was waiting to talk to you, Mr. Levy."

"Is something wrong?"

"I just wanted to say that I appreciate it, sir, that you said I could come along." There was hesitation. "And that I lied to you that first night."

"Lied?"

"Yes. When I first had supper at your house, last year. My father *was* a fighter pilot, and he did die in an air raid, but my mother's not who I said she was."

"What do you mean?"

"She's a Carnegie from Simonstown. She gave me up when I was born."

"I see."

"Elspeth, who's sort of been like a mom to me, and my father never married, but they tried to give me the feeling of it, I suppose. Elspeth's a cashier at OK Bazaars."

"Jeremy, I —"

"When my father died, Elspeth moved to Woodstock.

Her boyfriend lives with us."

I tell you my insides felt cold.

"Do you have other relatives?"

"An auntie in Jo'burg. She sends me a card at Christmastime."

My father didn't press the point.

I sank back into my pillow, feeling the same hollowness as the time Miss Thebus in Standard Three had told us Merle had died of TB and we all had to go to the funeral. I had called Merle *pisgat* because of her pee-smelling clothes, and couldn't stand the thought of being forced to go to church to look at her dead face.

I watched them there in the silvery light, my oppositionist father, my white-haired friend. What was it he said the Qur'an said? I couldn't remember, but something about spending out of your substance for orphans and those who asked.

"Do you think, Jeremy, that these figs will be ripe by the time we get back from the trip? My wife planted this tree five years ago, and every year these small little things come out and drop rock hard to the ground."

Of course, we never spoke about it, Jeremy and me. On the trip my heart swelled when I saw my mother drape his socks over a branch to dry, and I turned the chops on the *braai*, noticing my parents for the first time. Maybe one day one of them'll tell me about it and I won't have to wade through the Carnegies in the phone book.

❖

BILLIE CAN'T POO

IN A SMALL TOWN like Peterborough in the early seventies, you didn't meet many South Africans. But suddenly there she was at the desk Mr. Chapman's secretary used to occupy, plugged into the dictaphone, looking over a file. "Bitchy," some of the girls said, avoiding her in the lunch room. "Judgemental and uptight."

They were right. Everything that came out of her mouth was a biting remark. Canadians were insipid, ungrateful, unappreciative. They had to live in a country where you stood in the rain for a bus while an empty one for whites went by to understand the freedom they had.

The office played in a bowling league, and Sabah and her husband, Miles, were put on our team. There wasn't much chatter those first months — Sabah throwing mostly gutter balls, not good at any sports, she claimed. I saw Miles' reaction the day we finally sat down between sets and talked. Still, we did become friends, hard and fast by the end of the season when she threw a bad ball, costing us the game, and Miles had been unable to hold in his rage. She spoke of her marriage then. The problem wasn't infidelity, cheating, or physical abuse, but a lie. Six years ago he'd promised they would move to South

Africa, and she'd trusted him. In the end he just laughed. Canada was where *his* mother was now. Forget it, babe.

I didn't know Ella from Lena before meeting Sabah, but I took to going to the house on Saturday afternoons to listen to her great collection of jazz and stories of home. She'd grown up with the sounds of Satchmo, Gillespie and the Monk — both her brothers were sax players now — and South Africans had a passion for sambas, bossa novas, and blues. One Saturday I arrived to a van outside the house, Miles packing all his belongings into it. When the van had disappeared down the road, she turned to me. "I'm going home to catch my breath for a few weeks, Billie. Wanna come?"

When the plane descended over D.F. Malan in Cape Town, she burst out like a ripe tomato.

"Sabah, what's the matter?"

Snorting into the sleeve of her shirt, she pointed to the mountains below. "I don't cry when I leave, Billie. I cry when I come."

Fifty people or more were at the airport to meet us, with bags and parcels and flowers and a guava juice someone had popped into my hand, everyone talking at once.

The first problem, scarcely thirty minutes on South African soil, was who had first rights to us. Mrs. Dollie — she'd gone back to her maiden name — claimed that as she was the mother she deserved the honour of Sabah coming home to her, so the destination was Wynberg, and "please, everybody, we'll see you there." Mr. Solomon, Sabah's father, said that he had specially prepared a room with two single beds, that his ex-wife didn't

have first dibs and Sabah was going with him to Walmer
Estate. Sabah's eldest brother, Riaaz, chimed in, saying
he was married now, had a big house, he wanted his sister with him. All this in the parking lot while cousins and
uncles and aunts waited to hear in which direction they
should point their cars. In the end, Sabah refused to go
anywhere and they finally agreed to one day with her
mother, one day with her father, weekends left open for
brothers, cousins and friends.

Mrs. Dollie's house was a lovely, whitewashed,
Spanish-style bungalow, chock full of antiques, African
rugs and artifacts, a kidney-shaped pool in the yard. She
couldn't swim, and had once fallen in the pool trying to
manouevre an avocado from a branch overhead. Two
people had to get her out even though the water was only
six feet deep.

"Don't stand near the edge, Billie," she cautioned me
later on. "They wait for you to stand there in your nice
clothes, then throw you in. Riaaz is just a terrible boy.
When this house was first built and the Imam came to
bless it, he knocked the Imam into the pool, clothes and
all."

Riaaz laughed.

"Don't laugh," Mrs. Dollie said. "The poor man's fez
was floating in the deep end, he almost drowned."

"Serves him right for telling us Muslims shouldn't
have pools."

Mrs. Dollie lived alone with Rudwaan, and there was
ample room, she said, she didn't know why Sabah still
had to go and sleep at her father's as if he deserved equal
time. The kitchen was noisy with aunts and neighbours
pouring tea, all waiting to hear about Canada, Mrs.
Dollie clucking like an excited hen over her brood.

That first night, watching Sabah with her family, the bossa nova rhythms of Stan Getz swelling and dipping over the laughter and noise, tea coming non-stop, plates constantly refilled with jam tarts, custard rolls and chocolate eclairs, I felt drawn in as if by a wave. No one was concerned about weight, and I watched enviously as brothers and cousins and friends just dug in, later rounding it all off with chicken curry and rice and mango juice. There was no order, no rules.

"You know, I've never heard a girl swear like that," a striking man who had sat quietly all evening, suddenly said.

"Really?" Sabah responded caustically. "And who're you?"

"Your future brother-in-law, Suleiman Adams. My sister, Somaya over there, is engaged to your brother, Rudwaan." Rudwaan was a carpenter, a good-looking boy of twenty-six, Somaya, the twenty-one-year-old daughter of a wealthy advocate living in BoKaap.

"A doctor at the clinic," Mrs. Dollie said proudly.

"I've never heard the eff word go with so many things," he said, fascinated by Sabah. "I can't believe it, Mrs. Dollie, that you have a daughter like this." The poor boy.

He came to the Dollie house several times, taking us out for scenic drives and dinner to Constantia Nek, trying to get Sabah's attention. But Sabah didn't consider herself single yet, had her own agenda and wasn't interested. That didn't mean she didn't tease the hell out of Suleiman Adams over the next month.

When the last guest finally left around two, and I was starting to feel dizzy from the long flight and all the excitement, Sabah said she was taking her mother's car to

Sea Point — she always went to this place when she came. So off we went, in the middle of the night, up the mountainous De Waal Drive, overlooking the city and harbour lights, comforted by the smoothness of the Citroën on the winding road. Fifteen minutes later we arrived on Beach Road to the crashing sea, the rich salt air filling the car. On our left was the mountain dotted with houses overlooking miles of dark surf; on the road, cafes, restaurants, more houses, and apartment blocks.

We came to a lonely spot with a bench, and she stopped. The bench was wet, and in front of it was a railing along the boardwalk. Below the railing the waves rolled thunderously over the rocks, splashing over our heads. I saw a huge spray of foam rise up and quickly ran back to the car.

"This is it, Billie! This is it!" she laughed, holding on to the railing, turning her nose to the night sky, as the sea washed down over her head. The girl was mad, I thought, watching her through the window. She finally got back in with sopping jeans, soaking the plush seats of the Citroën. We drove back without a word.

Hardly six hours later the phone rang, her father asking what time we were coming, he was planning a *braai* for his side of the family, expecting us no later than two. Rudwaan drove us to Walmer Estate, where the house and yard were crowded with people excited to see Sabah, Riaaz standing barechested in jeans in front of a smoking brick barbecue turning sausages and chops. The noise was deafening. Mr. Solomon had four Dobermans — his built-in alarm system, he said — and the Solomon men were such a loud bunch you could hear them at the store. Once, the story went, while listening to a boxing match on the kitchen radio, the dogs panting at their feet, they were making such a noise, burglars had come in through the bedroom window and stolen all the blankets from the beds.

The morning after the *braai*, Mrs. Dollie was on the phone saying she missed us, Sabah had been at her father's long enough. And so it went with phone calls every morning from either Mrs. Dollie or Mr. Solomon.

When we'd been in Cape Town three days and I still hadn't gone to the bathroom, I asked Mrs. Dollie if she had a laxative. She gave me a dose of castor oil, squeezing the juice of an orange on my tongue afterwards. "Best thing, Billie," she said. "I always gave Sabah and her brothers this when they were small."

It was Saturday, and Riaaz and his wife, Saliyah, came over for breakfast.

"And how're the Canadians?"

"Billie can't poo," Mrs. Dollie said.

"Billie can't poo? What do you mean, Billie can't poo? Billie, can't you poo?"

I didn't know where to hide. "No."

"Did you go since you came?" he asked, forking a grilled kidney into his mouth.

"No."

"Billie sit vas," Mrs. Dollie said.

"What's that?"

"My mother said you sat it into a cement block on the plane."

Everyone laughed.

"What's the matter with you two," Sabah said. "Leave my friend alone, guys."

"Yes," Saliyah said. "You're acting very foolish, Riaaz."

"What did you give her, Mom?" he asked.

"Castor oil."

"Castor oil? Billie needs a bomb, not castor oil. I'll go to the chemist afterwards and get her something."

"Wait till tomorrow," Mrs. Dollie said. "I gave her two teaspoons. We don't want Billie having accidents in her pants. Aren't you going to Ceres with Toyer tomorrow?"

"The day after. We're going to daddy's this afternoon. Remember?"

"I don't see why your father should get so many turns."

"We'll give you a lift," Riaaz said.

"Listen, don't you be in a hurry to take them away. I gave them the other car. Your father can wait his blinking turn."

"The Volksie? That car's dangerous."

"Well, they're not getting the Citroën again. You should see what they did to the seats," and she thumped Sabah on the head. "If they don't like it, Rudwaan can take them when he gets up. And he's another one. Came in four o'clock this morning."

"My mother's nagging, Billie, because soon Rudwaan's gone too. He's getting married in June."

"He can be gone *now*, Billie, for all I care. Leaving his work clothes on the bathroom floor and never making up his bed. And I have to lick his arse to put the chemicals in the pool or vacuum it. I won't take his side one bit if Somaya complains. Rudwaan!" she shouted towards the back of the house, "Get up!"

"She's a pretender," Riaaz said. "Rudwaan's her favourite. Tell her, mom, how you always brag that he's the only one who remembers mother's day. My mother's such a patsy for a phone call and chocolates, even if he takes the twenty right out of her purse."

We arrived at the house on the hill late in the afternoon.

Mr. Solomon was drinking tea with two men on the *stoep*, playing dominoes.

"Billie!"

I'd become his favourite.

"Where were you yesterday? Did you go out? We were waiting for you to play cards." I'd taught them how to play scat.

"We went to town with Rudwaan."

"And Friday we're going with Toyer to Ceres," Sabah said. "Billie wants to see a tobacco farm. Toyer also needs a new kitchen girl. The one they had got pregnant from the gardener."

"What're you going with Toyer for? He's no relative of yours. Now everyone wants to jump in. You're only here for a month, girl."

"Don't be selfish, daddy. We're all going. Rudwaan, Somaya, maybe even Suleiman."

"That drip?"

"You're just jealous 'cause none of your children are doctors."

"Billie, have you seen that boy? He sits so upright, you can boil an egg in his bum."

"Mr. Solomon!" He knew how to work a crowd.

"That's right, Billie. All that studying's turned him into a prune, even I have a better sense of humour than him. So, what do you think of our beautiful country, Billie? Tell Mr. Lawrence and Mr. Vermaak what you think."

"Well, Mr. Solomon, I didn't see anyone with beads and feathers around their ankles running in the street yet."

He had an infectious laugh.

"So that's what they think of us over there."

"Billie has a problem," Riaaz said.

"A problem?"

"Billie can't poo."

"Billie can't poo? My goodness, nasty. Why can't you poo, Billie?"

"I don't know," I said, wishing for cramps.

"When was the last time?"

"In Canada," Riaaz laughed.

"Canada! Billie, you can poison yourself. You have a nerve to come and contaminate our land."

I tell you my face was red most days.

"Don't make fun of my friend," Sabah said, "She already had castor oil."

"My wife has some brown pills," Mr. Vermaak said. "I can pop over to the house later on and get some. Mr. Solomon knows she always had that problem with open bowels."

"No," Mr. Lawrence said. "Eat lots of pineapple, man, that's the best. Don't they have pineapples in Canada?"

"Of course they have pineapples in Canada. How can Mr. Lawrence then be so stupid?"

"Aagh, their pineapples are not like ours. Listen to me — what's your name? Billie? Listen to me, Billie. Forget all these remedies. Just eat pineapple tonight. No meat and rice. And pineapple again in the morning. I guarantee you'll go."

"Does Mr. Lawrence then want her to turn into a pineapple?" Mr. Solomon said. "Look at her, she already looks a little yellow around the gills."

They burst out laughing, Mr. Solomon leading the pack.

"Don't worry, Billie, I have a good remedy for open bowels," he said. "I've got something in the kitchen that's going to work the trick. I made it four days ago."

"And if Mr. Solomon's ginger beer doesn't move you," Mr. Lawrence said, "nothing will."

"That's right, Billie. Then we might as well take you in the van to Groote Schuur."

And they burst out all over again.

"I told you," Sabah said. "My family's not well."

"Come, Billie, let's go inside and have some ginger beer. What kind of a name is Billie, anyway? The name Billie in this country always comes with a pair of horns."

"You're too much, Mr. Solomon."

At the Dollie house, everything was spotless and in its place, the radio low, the music off at sunset for half an hour to respect maghrib prayers. You ate on time and you prayed on time. At the Solomon house there were sand prints from Dobermans, dirty ashtrays, dog bowls, piles of old newspapers next to the condensed milk and sugar on the kitchen counter, card games and music continuing "right through the *waghdoe*." No one prayed and no one felt guilty.

When we were there just a week, a relative died. After the funeral, ten of us were back around the huge table in the Solomon kitchen feeling depressed and someone suggested gin rummy to cheer us up.

"No," Sabah said. "We have to have respect. How can we play cards when someone just died? The man's hardly cold."

"Aagh, what," Mr. Solomon said, "Boeta Braim would *want* us to enjoy ourselves. Riaaz, get the cards. Somaya, put on the kettle for tea. Let's have a few hands for Boeta Braim."

We went into the oak trim kitchen — everything in there he'd built with his own hands, he said, here was the missing thumb to prove it — and came upon two huge paraffin tins on the floor. He lifted the lid and the ginger aroma hit my nose.

Riaaz put out eight glasses, and Mr. Solomon took a mug and dipped it into the fizzing brew, pouring the potent brown liquid into a glass, giving Sabah a first taste.

"Whoofff!" she said, blinking. "This kicks!"

I took a sip and felt the fire rip down my throat.

"What did I tell you, hey?" he smacked his lips. "No later than tomorrow, Billie, you'll sing the national anthem."

But nothing happened, and we spent the next morning playing cards in our pyjamas and gowns with friends who had come to find out which horses he was favouring for the jackpot, Mr. Solomon continuing to pour the ginger beer into my glass. At lunch time the horn sounded outside, and there was Mrs. Dollie in her polished Citroën, waiting to take us to Wynberg.

"Your mother's getting mighty brave driving that car up my street every day," Mr. Solomon said to no one in particular. "I wouldn't be surprised if that woman still has a crush on me. Ever since I saw her in Salt River just before you girls arrived from Canada, she's getting brave. I tell you, Billie, she couldn't get out of that car fast enough, preening like a peacock, almost falling over her feet with nervousness."

"Oh, stop it, daddy," Sabah said. "You think everyone's in love with you."

We jumped into the car, pyjamas and all, and then had to listen to Mrs. Dollie's version of how she had bumped into the old goat in Salt River, and him purposely parking his van behind her to have a better look. The man had to get over his ridiculousness at fifty.

It was a scorching day. We decided to spend the afternoon playing scrabble by the pool.

"It's a heat wave out there," Mrs. Dollie shouted from the kitchen window. "I'm not coming out. You girls can come in if you want something to drink."

"I'm taking off my bather, Billie," Sabah said, pulling the straps off her shoulder, stepping out of it, jumping into the pool. I sat for a few minutes watching her head break the surface, then her bum as she dove down again.

Her mother, despite what she'd said, came out with tall glasses of chilled guava juice on a tray.

"Mom, you have to keep watch," Sabah said, her head above the water.

"Why?"

"I'm skinny dipping, mom."

"Skinny dipping? What nonsense is this? Is that what you learned in Canada? To swim without clothes on? If my mother was alive now, she'd die."

"Don't be such a prude, mom, it's just us. No one'll see."

"God sees." She pretended to be cross, and went back inside, nodding her head.

Sabah got out, and after a few minutes in the sun, said, "Ever pee standing up, Billie?"

"What?" I'd given up figuring her out.

"Yes." She walked around the pool to the grass on the other side. "You stand like this, and you lean your leg slightly inwards, then you let the pee run down your thigh." And she closed her eyes to the sun, smiling like the devil as the pee trailed down her leg into the grass.

"God, this feels good! It's such a nice warm feeling against your leg. And it goes straight from you into the ground. Don't you have to pee?"

Swimming without bathing suits, peeing on your own foot? Was this the frigid bitch everyone at the office said had a peg up her arse?

Then we saw Suleiman Adams coming through the garage. Mrs. Dollie must've been performing noon prayers when he knocked on the front door. I think Sabah registered his presence and her nakedness the same time as me. I expected her to jump in the pool, but she remained, smiling innocently.

"You're naked," he finally blurted.

"Yeah, well, you just walked in. Wait till my mother sees you in the yard here with us."

I rolled her towel in a bundle and threw it over. It was a foot or so short of landing on the other side and she could've caught it, but she let it fall in the pool.

"Well, I — maybe I should —"

"Throw my bather, Billie."

This she caught, and pulled up, up her thighs, wriggling into the wet suit, as Suleiman tried hard to keep his eyes on the trees.

We left early the next morning for Ceres, six of us jammed into Toyer's hump-backed Volvo. I didn't know where we were going to fit in a new kitchen girl. My stomach had rumbled a few times, giving me hope, and I was a little uncomfortable sitting between Sabah and Somaya in the back.

We stopped at a lovely spot at the foot of the pass, and Somaya took out a hamper from the trunk.

"Salmon sandwiches, anyone? Mince pies?"

"Somaya makes good sandwiches," Rudwaan said.

"I'm having some really bad cramps," I told Sabah.

"You have to go?"

"I don't know. It's all in my stomach still."

"You can't pick a better place than this, Billie. Right behind those trees. Once we get back in the car, it's mountain road all the way. There'll be no place to stop."

The cramps subsided a bit, and I had coffee and sandwiches with them.

Riaaz took out a joint. "*Skuif*, Billie?"

"Wait till Saliyah hears of this," Sabah said, taking a few heavy drags. "Whaaahh...," she breathed out, "we don't have this quality in Canada."

We all stood around *trekking skuif* — I was getting pretty good at the lingo — and I almost forgot about the cramps.

We got back in the car and headed up the pass.

Ten minutes later the cramps were back, moving with knife-like force into my bowels.

"Can you stop the car?"

"What is it, Billie?"

"It's an emergency. Please!"

"Oh, my word," Toyer said. "We can't stop here. Can you hold it in?"

"No," I almost screamed.

We were on a narrow road high up on the mountain with a two-foot gravel shoulder. When I looked out, I got dizzy seeing the bushes and rocks hundreds of feet below. Then I felt it come, and couldn't hold back.

"Please, stop, I have to get out!"

Toyer put on the turn signal, coming to an abrupt halt.

I climbed hastily over Somaya's legs and stood out on the gravel next to the car, ripping off my jeans. I didn't dare look over the cliff and didn't care about the cars coming up the hill, the wind blowing up my arse. The button didn't come undone fast enough, and I hit everything, including the tire of the car.

"Holy, fuck!" Sabah exclaimed, "she's doing it right next to the car. Do we have something in the back to cover her up?"

She went to the trunk, and got out an ugly brown blanket, which she draped around me while I squatted and hit the road. On and on, five minutes, ten minutes, the breeze waffling my *poz*, everyone in the car politely busying themselves.

"Look at these fuckers staring. What're you looking at? Drive on!" she shouted.

"I'm sorry, Sabah. I'm so ashamed. And I don't have any tissues."

"Somaya," she thumped on the window. "Some napkins, please."

"Napkins?"

"Serviettes!"

"We used them when we had the sandwiches."

I was in a strange country with my arse over a cliff, shitting all over my jeans. Who would believe this story?

"Isn't there any paper in the car?" she asked again.

"Only Riaaz' *Times*. Do you want that?"

"I didn't read it yet," Riaaz shouted.

"Don't get *kak* now, Riaaz," Sabah got nasty. "Hand it over."

"I'll give you the property guide," he said, "I don't read that. Or do you want sports?"

"I don't care what fucking section you give, just give it! You want us to die out here waiting?"

"What about my jeans?" I lamented. "I can't keep them on. Oh my God, this is so embarrassing."

"Billie, it's just us," she handed me strips of newspaper. "Take off your jeans. You'll have to sit in this blanket till we get home."

I was there for all the passing cars to gawk at, stepping out of my pants, my foot scraping both the jeans and my mess over the cliff. My bum burning like someone had taken sandpaper to it, feeling crampy and soiled, wrapped like a mummy from the waist down, I got back into the car.

"My father and his bladdy ginger beer," Riaaz said. "You okay, Billie?"

"Wat nou, mense?" Toyer asked.

"Turn the car around, man. Picnic's over. We can't go with Billie in a blanket to a farm."

Mr. Solomon, when he heard the news, gloated all over again about the potency of his home brew, and for days there were enquiries about my bowels, and advice on follow-up maintenance. Mr. Lawrence brought a box of pineapples and a few packets of dried fruit to the house, just in case, and even Suleiman brought prunes.

There was only one incident to remind me where I was. Sabah and I went shopping in the business area of Athlone and returned to find the car standing on four bricks, the tires stolen in broad daylight right in front of the Athlone Police Station.

The constable on duty, a dark-skinned man with a friendly smile, pointed us to the other side of the wooden partition.

"Over there, please."

"I want to report a theft," Sabah said.

"Over there, miss," he said again. "You're standing in the section for non-whites."

"I'm not white."

"Please, miss," he smiled patiently, "if you go over

there, someone can take your complaint."

"I'm not white, and I don't want to go over there."

"What's the address?"

"My mother lives in Athlone. Belgravia Road. Now, can I continue? Our car was parked outside, and —"

"Miss, look, I'm sorry. If you and your friend — and don't tell me she's from Athlone too — if the two of you want to go over there, Constable Van Rijn can look after you."

"Can you believe this, Billie? They can't make up their minds what the fuck I am."

I didn't know what she was talking about.

In the end we went back outside, Sabah calling Rudwaan from the public phone to come and sort it all out.

A few days before our departure I noticed Mrs. Dollie no longer fought over Sabah, and in fact, seemed to be pushing her away. Coming into the kitchen early one morning, I caught her deep in thought at the sink, looking through the window at the trees in the yard. Sabah had warned me. Her mother went into mourning while she was still there.

"And what are your plans today, Mrs. Dollie?"

"Oh, nothing my girl," she said softly, her eyes a little watery. "I think I'll stay home and make some pastries for next week. Are you missing Canada?"

"I miss my mother, yes."

"What's a mother, hey? All children are the same. You know, Billie, my mother died six months after Sabah left in 1968. I still miss her today. Can you believe that? A grown woman like me. Sometimes when I think of Sabah so far away, I cry for my mother, and I cry for Sabah. My mother always said, you can have ten sons, it doesn't equal one girl. My sons are good sons, Billie, don't get me wrong. But sons take wives, move on with their own families. Daughters are yours no matter who they're with. Do you have any brothers, Billie?"

"I'm an only child."

"Shame. That must be lonely for you."

"I'm used to it, Mrs. Dollie. My mother and I are friends."

I sat with her in the kitchen a long time, letting her talk her heart out.

In Walmer Estate Mr. Solomon also was saying hardly anything.

"I'm not coming to the airport on Friday," he mumbled one night. I had come to enjoy sitting in the kitchen reading the evening newspaper with him.

"It's all right," Sabah said.

"And don't still drive here when you leave. I'll say goodbye on the phone."

"Yes, Daddy."

Then his tone changed and he sounded cross. "I don't know when you're coming home, Sabah. You've been there eight years now."

"We've gone over this before, Daddy. I have children there."

"Yes, you have children, we all have children."

"Their father's Canadian. They love him."

Nothing more was said.

The day arrived, and Sabah tried all day to get him on the telephone, but he was nowhere to be found.

Our bags were checked in, and we started to edge towards the metal gate. All around us, sad faces looked on, people sticking chocolates and gifts into our hands, and I noticed a strange hardness in Sabah. There was no laughter, or tears in her eyes, just a vacantness. Her mother was crying into several hankies, supported by Somaya and Saliya on the bench.

"All right, Mom," she said, "Till next time, hey?"

Mrs. Dollie just blew harder into her hankie and went to pieces in front of everyone.

"Stop it, Mom. Don't let me go like this."

"Go, Sabah," Rudwaan pushed her off. "Leave Mummy with us."

"Look after her, Saliya. You too, Somaya. Don't forget to visit when you and Rudwaan get married, hey?" Then we stepped through the metal gate, and Sabah became someone else.

We spoke briefly of our jobs, not a word about the people we'd just left, and she went to sleep. Somewhere over central Africa, I started to cry for no reason. When I didn't stop and couldn't tell Sabah what was wrong because I myself didn't know, she called the stewardess who took me to the crew's quarters where the purser gave me a tranquilizer.

I don't know what that was all about, if the madness had touched my blood. I don't know if it was the family just swallowing me in, the sea air, or Sabah's recklessness. I just know that the sudden withdrawal and silence affected me like a child who'd lost his mother's hand in the park.

"They robbed me, Billie," was all she said when we touched down on the icy runway at Toronto. "They robbed me, those fucking bastards."

❖

Don't Mention It

MY GRANDMOTHER WAS COMING, and for weeks I listened
to the excitement in my mother's voice to Marcy on the
telephone. Out went my panties with the holes and my
brother's heelless socks, kitchen cupboards were cleaned
out and wiped, cans and jars neatly stacked with labels
all facing the front. I only knew my father's mother, who
took us to the Sheraton to hunt for Easter eggs and
bought us ribbed sweaters at Christmastime, and dreaded
meeting this other grandmother who was coming all the
way from the jungle to see what her Canadian grandchil-
dren were about.

I'd heard stories about upbringing in South Africa.
"My mother would put chillies in my mouth if I said
damn" or "I'd get the hard end of the feather duster on
my knuckles if I took what wasn't mine." I knew my
brother, whose mouth constantly runneth over, wouldn't
have much of a chance, and I was counting on him to
take most of the heat. But I was curious, anxious for
clues about my own mom, who I had long ago decided
defied regular description. My brother and I were the
only children in Richmond Hill whose mom had a haircut
like that rifleman with his boot on an elephant's head

advertising cigarettes in *TV Guide*, who never stood up for *O Canada*, popping peanuts while eyes burned holes into the back of our heads. I was really curious to see what kind of mother she had.

Finally the afternoon arrived, and my brother and I stood in our pressed clothes at the airport waiting for my grandmother to come through the electronic door, my mother leaning against a pillar reading one of her short-story books. At my friend Louise's house there were fashion magazines in the toilet, in ours, Nadine Gordimer and Alice Munro, and on mom's bed where dad used to sleep, a stack of *Quarry* and *Grain*.

I knew the minute I saw this big woman in a cream, tailored suit with this black velvet turban sitting a little crooked on her head, a bright orange patch of hair sticking out the left side, that this was my famous gran. You didn't have to be an expert or anything to know just from that patch that no one in their right mind would pick a colour like that. Right there a piece of the puzzle fit.

I was quiet that first day chomping on a stick of dried meat called biltong, listening to my mother shamelessly ransack my grandmother's brain for news of cousins and uncles and old friends, watching the poor woman fight to stay awake — she'd waited fourteen hours on a plastic chair for a connecting flight in Rome. Finally my mother showed her to the extra bed she'd put in my room upstairs. I hadn't looked forward to sharing, but was fascinated by this big woman on the edge of the bed folding everything in a neat pile on the chair, her suitcase open at her feet like at an Indian bazaar displaying chocolates and dried fruit and slippers and guavas from the tree in her yard stuck between rolled clothing, strangely comforted by the pleasantness of her eau de cologne.

"My girl, can you take my nightie out? It should be
right on top. Under those Cadbury's, I think."

"Yes, Gran," I fairly hopped out of bed. "This one?" I
held the pink brushed nylon one up.

"That's it. Thank you."

"You're welcome."

"You're welcome?"

"It means, like, well, when someone says thank you,
you say you're welcome."

"Oh, sort of like, don't mention it."

"Don't mention it?"

"Yes, don't mention it, it's a pleasure. You can also just
say, pleasure. Someone says, thank you, and you say,
pleasure."

"I like don't mention it better, because sometimes,
Gran, don't you think, it's not always a pleasure?"

She laughed.

"You're right. I think that's why we say don't mention
it most of the time. It's not always a pleasure. Smart
Canadian *tutus* I have, I see."

"Thank you, Gran."

"You're welcome."

We both got a kick out of that, and I got into bed, gran
pulling the covers up to my chin, kissing me on the head.
I had already decided that since Juaa was mom's pet —
she denied this strenuously, saying he's just her first child
— that I would do everything to get myself in good with
gran. I knew of course, like I always knew when people
met my brother for the first time, that my grandmother
too would be helpless under his spell. And she was,
although she was a lot smarter than mom at keeping it in
the corner of her heart. But I had other strengths, and
given time, knew I could prove myself. If there was one

thing I knew like I knew I hated Gideon Cohn in my class, it was that my brother wouldn't be able to hold himself in for a whole two months.

When two weeks had passed, and I had warmed to the smells of puddings and fudge, because gran had a thing about being idle and was always *prittling* in the kitchen whipping up treats or in the living room with her feather duster — she'd brought one in her suitcase — I came to the conclusion that grandmothers were more interesting than moms. Of course she wasn't anything as glamorous as my other grandmother — mom browned that orange hair fast and virtually wrenched away the eyebrow pencil, giving her eye shadow instead — but then my Toronto grandmother didn't know baking powder from flour and bought cheesecake from a German baker, taking it out of the box before visitors arrived. That's not to say though that gran's eyes and ears weren't in the best working order and that she didn't spot our little mistakes. Juaa got a hard taste when he came home with his bat one day after supper had been on the table an hour and was asked if he thought he was at an hotel. For a minute I thought he was going to roll those big eyes and turn on that smile that all those ten-year-olds liked, but he must've pitched some bad balls because he mumbled something unintelligible and went to the bathroom to wash his hands. "Gran's talking to you," my mother said, under pressure to exert some control. "Whoa! I'd better listen then." Mom threatened him with no supper, something she'd never done before, and my grandmother rolled those meat cylinders out of her seat, disappointment thick in her voice. "I never thought I'd have a rude grandchild." That was all it took.

My brother has this terrible problem — he can't

function if he thinks you don't love him, even though he
doesn't shut his mouth when he should, and the next
morning when she woke up, there it was on her folded
slacks, a box of Smarties and a note. That the box was
half empty didn't matter, gran was knocked over by the
thought. Were we girls really such suckers for chocolates
from Shoppers Drug Mart? When he returned from
school she'd made a trifle and he invited three of his
friends to come and meet his South African gran. From
that day on it didn't matter what he did — except
backchatting mom, of course — gran would just nod her
head, and say, "Aagh."

Around this time I noticed mom, who had a rule about
wanting everything in its place, getting edgy with gran.
Gran came from a country, she said, where people
knocked on your door for a slice of bread, and couldn't
throw anything out. So leftovers appeared everywhere.
In one of mom's china cups in the cupboard was a handful of tangerine pips turning the bottom of the cup brown
that gran was drying out to take home and plant because
"Florida *naartjies* were sweet," in the fridge an uncovered
saucer with half a boiled egg smelling up the cheese, a
slice of tomato, a half-eaten muffin, and farther back,
behind the diet margarine, a chicken wing in wax paper
not properly sealed, and crumbly sponge cake from the
week before. Gran would begin an Oh Henry, lose inter-
est, and save it for later on. The fruit bowl in the kitchen
had candy wrappers stuck between the oranges and
bananas, gran never finishing anything.

"Mom, what're you saving these bits and pieces for?"
My mother would try to keep the sting out of her voice.
"Throw it out if you can't finish it, please. I'm not short
on tomatoes and eggs, and chocolates you can do with-

out." Personally, I didn't know what all the fuss was about. Gran was a pack rat and had probably been a caterpillar collector like me. And there was no mystery any more where I got the habit of saving my meat for last on my plate till my potatoes and peas were gone. In any event, gran would look at mom with doleful eyes, nod, then find a different hiding place. Mom of course knew nothing about the stash of teabags growing mold in a bowl under the bed. Gran was saving them to mix with her henna paste, for she had every intention of going back to being a burgundy blonde.

One afternoon watching her iron sheets and under-wear I told her mom just folded the sheets and smoothed out the panties with her hand.

"Your mom never wore creased panties or petticoats, but I guess she's too busy now. But you put this on after your bath tonight, and tell me if it doesn't feel good against your skin. Women put on a little perfume some-times to cheer themselves up, you know. A nicely pressed blouse or slip can do the same thing."

"Really, Gran?"

"Really. But I notice people here don't care very much how they look. Not too many creases in pants or pleated skirts. Maybe that's why they're so out of sorts. Even your mother doesn't iron her jeans."

"You only notice mom's clothes now? She gets into trouble all the time at work because she hates wearing a dress."

"But she wears dresses all the time."

"Not Fridays, Gran. Fridays she wears jeans."

"Jeans in an office?"

"She says she doesn't have to go in every day, and if they want her to bring in the business she's written

Thursday night, it's jeans or they can wait till Monday. Of course, the manager wants the numbers on the board so he has no choice because mom writes the most business, and if you say anything to mom, you know how she is, she just won't write anything at all even though it means we'll all be starving to death."

"Your mother's always been a mischief maker."

"Tell me Gran, did they really move her from Sub A to Sub B when she started school?"

"Yes. And when she was ten, she was Spring Queen. Make your gran a nice cup of tea and I'll tell you about the time someone pulled her plait and she broke the girl's arm."

"Gran, you're telling lies!"

"She didn't mean to, of course, but there it was, the girl called her whitey, pulled her hair, they rolled to the floor, and when they were separated by the teacher who'd come back into the class, your mother's mouth was bleeding and the girl's arm was broken."

"Were they expelled?"

"No. But I got a call from the principal."

"Did mom tell you what happened?"

"She never said a word, made up some story about her teeth. The tea, my girl? Do you remember how?"

"I boil the water, and make sure it boils."

"Then you take that small white teapot with the pink flowers and put some hot water in it to warm it up."

"I know the rest, Gran. You want the thin cup with the gold rim, you don't drink tea out of mugs. And three teaspoons of loose tea in the pot."

"You forgot something."

"Boil the milk in the microwave."

"Right."

I made it, hot and strong the way she liked, and put the two china cups next to the dainty plate of marzipan cookies she'd set out. I prayed my brother wouldn't come crashing through the door, and gran dropping everything to make him something to eat; there were things I wanted to know. But I'd hardly reached for a marzipan when I heard the bicycles slam against the wall, the front door open, and three of them tumble into the house. "Gran, you remember Gregory and Mike? My grandmother makes the best grilled-cheese sandwiches, guys! Can you make us some, Gran?" And before she could answer, they charged up the stairs to his room, our little tea party at an end.

Gran was restless and we were always out. "You're just a street Arab, Mom," my mother would say when gran got fidgety. "Well, I didn't come here to sit on my bum, man. I want to see Canada. Take me somewhere in the car." So if it wasn't a movie or a restaurant or a drive to Niagara Falls, it was scouring the stores in the mall. And a most painstaking thing it was, as gran had to examine every label, every price, to compare with the clothes back home.

The first time we took her to Bulk Barn, it was like witnessing someone who'd never been to a zoo with more than five animals. Gran saw all the barrels and bins and said that they could never have such a place in South Africa, people would just dip their hands in and steal. She loved the idea of taking as little or as much in a plastic bag, and not being stuck with a five-pound bag of flour when you only wanted to make a few scones. Admiring the faith the shop owners had in their customers, I saw her stand a bit too long in one of the aisles, and thought I'd investigate. Gran took a plastic bag and dipped her hand into the chocolate-coated almonds, putting five or six in the bag. Then, when we were pushing the cart down the aisle and no one was around, she removed the almonds from the bag and put them in her pocket, leaving the empty bag in the cart. I was stunned.

In the car going home, she took them out of her pocket and gave one to me and to mom. My mother said she didn't remember paying for almonds, and Gran said she'd taken them as samples to see if she wanted to buy some the next time. "But that's stealing," my mother said, "you taught us stealing was wrong."

"G'wan, man," gran popped an almond into her mouth, "they won't miss two or three. Look how much you paid for those cashew nuts."

I must say, I liked gran's philosophy. Not long after that, I'm sorry to say, mom tried the same stunt with those big dates she'd always had her eye on. The difference was, whereas gran eventually bought a few pounds of the almonds to take back to South Africa, mom just put three dates into her pocket — not even bothering with the plastic bag — every time she went to Bulk Barn.

As one week slipped into another, and I saw the suitcase slowly fill up, I dreaded the end of August. Sometimes when I watched from the other end of the dining room table where I sat with my books, I caught gran staring out at the lake. She was missing home, anxious to return, and I loved her for not sharing this with mom. Gran knew. My mother didn't want to be here but she was here because we were here and we had to be here because we were Canadian, my father said, and no one could take us away.

"What you sitting looking so glum for, Mom?"

"I'm just thinking, Sabah my girl. You live so far away."

"Yes, Mom." And I picked up that thing in her voice. "Are you ever going to come home?"

"One day, Mom." She put a plate of cookies on the table, going back into the kitchen for the tea tray and a new short-story book.

Gran understood. When they were like this, there was nothing I could do. When mom would be the child and gran would be the mom they communicated in a language of silences alien to me.

The last week of her stay gran decided to make balloon curtains for the whole house and she and my mother went over to this material place and aggravated the lady there for almost the whole afternoon. I hid behind the crêpe de chine as I listened to my grandmother work out the lengths and widths of lace and taffeta from a scrap of paper she rooted out of her bag, the poor Chinese lady struggling to keep up as they decided first on one then another colour, then dragging her to the other side of the room for something else. My mother had never had a needle in her hand but because she had now laid out three hundred dollars for a sewing machine, while gran was ordering the lady about, she was paging through pattern books fired up with how much money she could save. I think I saw the lady cringe when mom looked at the name tag on her dress, and said, "Big San, you've been so helpful. If I have any trouble, I'm coming straight to you." We left laden like camels with materials and zippers and enough patterns to keep mom through Thanksgiving the next year.

The living room took on a new appearance: the oak table was cleared of the elaborate flower arrangement and replaced with the Elna and metres and metres of dark green taffeta gran fed through the machine, the

∂tzzz ∂tzzz ∂tzzz very soothing as it mixed with CJRT, the sun spilling onto mom on the carpet where she was bent over a pattern like a girl cutting pictures out of a colouring book.

"Oprah's coming on, why don't we take a break?"

Gran had become fascinated with afternoon talk shows. I'd already had to grapple with a new word when gran had said "kaffir," and mom almost washed out her mouth, when here was another.

One of the ladies on the panel said she'd never had an orgasm, and gran asked what an orgasm was.

"What do you mean, what's an orgasm, Mom?"

"Well, I mean — do I know about these things?"

"What do you mean you don't know? At fifty-six you don't know what an orgasm is?"

I could see that ridge hardening between gran's eyes and wished someone would fill me in.

"Well, you don't have to excite your liver about it and stop mentioning my age."

"But Mom, you were married, for heaven's sake!"

Gran put her foot down with a vengeance on the treadle and fed the material through the machine.

"Do we have all these people coming on television in South Africa, spilling their guts, educating us? I don't need a man in my bed, and I'm sorry I blinkingwill asked."

I went into the kitchen, made a pot of tea and took the tray into the lion's den where Oprah was still philosophizing.

"You want sweetener or real sugar, Gran?"

"Real sugar, please," she said, knowing this would sour mom, who'd tried to cut her size with grapefruit and oatbran and twenty-minute workouts, that gran, caught up in mom's mania to be thin, stood every morning on the bathroom scale with gown and slippers waiting to see the pounds drop off. Of course it didn't make a dent in those rolling thighs, and when the needle seemed stuck at a hundred and seventy, she said the seven pounds lost had gone straight from her face and ate real breakfasts when mom left for work.

"Strong and hot, just the way I like it," she smiled. "Thank you."

"Pleasure, Gran."

Mom shot me a look that was hard to gauge, but was properly chastised, let me say. Gran could've stuck match sticks into avocado pits on the kitchen sill, she wouldn't have said anything.

The day of departure we drove like mourners to the airport. After the plane was swallowed up by the clouds, I had my first rub with loneliness, and a whole new fix on mom. Mom wasn't such a strange bird. Not after you met gran. Struggling to break free from the pattern that had strangled her mother's life, she wanted us independent, but not so that we thought we didn't need love, 'cause that was mom's problem now. She didn't read novels, she said, because that manipulated her time. *I was manipulated by the law*, won't be by a man. Relationships were short stories, good reads, where characters were lost on the moors or faded into sunsets.

My beloved grandmother came again in '89 with her feather duster and orange hair, her bread puddings and foreign jive. By this time of course Louise had had an orgasm in Greg's car, and I knew all about how gran had missed nothing at all.

FOR THE SMELL
OF THE SEA

THE FIRST TIME I MET EZZ she was lying in five inches of water in an old porcelain tub. "Go in," Hans, her sixty-year-old artist lover, said. "Everyone else is in there." So I followed Riaana into a narrow, white-tiled bathroom with this ponytailed man sitting on the toilet drinking beer, a very dark girl with long black hair and a short leather skirt on the edge of the bath smoking a joint, and this long-limbed amazon with an ugly stomach scar distorted under the water lying back with a glass in her hand, her partial denture in a cloud of Steradent next to a tray holding pills, hair straightener, ointments, a douche bag and a biscuit tin brimming with lipsticks, shadows and blush.

"Shit, it stinks in here."

"You *are* in a toilet, love," she said. "So you have the nerve to visit after not pitching up for Hans' show at the gallery? And who's this?"

"My cousin, Sabah, on holiday from Canada. Saa, this is Ezz, her cousin, Myrna, and Jeff."

There was no place to sit so I leaned against the wooden door careful not to skewer my neck on the nail, my eyes flitting briefly to the bubbles fizzing up between Ezz' legs, the smell punctuating the already rotten air.

"I love your hair," she turned to me. "Is it yours?"

"Yes," I laughed, surprised.

"Ezz hates her *kaffir* hair," Jeff said. "Can't accept her bushman beginnings."

"Oh shut up, you. And look who's talking. The boy who broke off his engagement because mommy said the girl's too black, the children might have *kroes* hair."

I tried to figure out the German artist who didn't mind this flagrancy and the very uninhibited girl in the tub. She was young, a decade younger than me, with lively eyes, full lips, a solid body with mango breasts. It wasn't hard to figure the buzz.

The door pushed against my back.

"Maurice is on the phone."

"You meet fishpaste Arthur yet?"

"You know I hate that name."

Arthur was tall, lantern-jawed, with pencilled eyes, an effeminate lilt in his voice.

"Maybe you'll stop blowing those old queens behind the Luxurama then. Look at that bruise in your neck."

"You're a bitch, Ezz."

"Oh, stop moaning like a baby, you puss. Tell Maurice I'll call him back. And wash your hands before you make the tea."

Arthur reversed out the door.

Ezz got up and Myrna handed her a towel. She let out a tiny smelly, fart.

"Stop it, Ezz."

"You know I can't help it."

"Stop blaming it on the operation."

"Shit, what did you eat? I'm outa here," Jeff said.

"Apricots. I'm giving a dinner party next Saturday, you must come." And with that she went out into the dining room where Hans was putting finishing touches to a painting, and led him into the bedroom leaving us standing there to entertain ourselves.

On the way home Riaana filled me in. Ezz was a fitness instructor at Lou's Gym, and had met Hans at a jazz session when she was sixteen, ten years ago, dropping out of school, moving right into his flat. People popped in at all hours, and it wasn't at all unusual on a weekend for someone to knock on Ezz' door at 4:00 a.m. — usually Jeff and Rollie (whom she still had to meet) — too drunk to drive home from a party up in the Kloof, needing a place to crash. Sometimes five people were heaped up in the same room with Ezz and Hans. Nothing going on, of course. For all Ezz' big mouth she was quite a prude. Her preoccupation was having other people smell her farts. Once she'd had a whole crew drinking tea and eating biscuits on her bed, and she got up and locked the door so they couldn't escape.

Myrna and Jeff, a story and a half. Supposedly just friends, Myrna, a radical, and co-publisher of an underground magazine, had a crush on Jeff. The problem was, Jeff was on the lookout for the right-complexioned girl to knock him off his feet and wanted only sex. One poker night at Ezz', after too much brandy and dagga, he *oetied* Myrna on the couch in front of everyone. In the morning Myrna was gone, Jeff passed out, his false teeth on the floor. "A mad group," Riaana said. "But, watch out, they're like attack dogs, they work in a pack."

I'd forgotten what Cape Town dinners were like, and

turned up with my cousin on Sussex Street in jeans and a check shirt. Ezz wore a black spandex stocking showing every dimpled curve, Myrna a silver-studded top and pants. Decked out and grand, jazz on the stereo, if it wasn't for Hans in his sandals and shorts, I would've felt like *asterpoester* before the ball.

"So what do you think of all this new stuff going on, the blacks coming into power?" Rollie Thomas asked. Rollie was Jeff's partner in crime, and had just brought them up to date on the elections scheduled for the following year.

"The sanctions worked."

"Have you been down to Sea Point yet? Camps Bay? You can't even get a spot to put up your umbrella or stretch your feet without getting sand kicked in your face. They're like animals, some of them, with their primus stoves and pots of food. Give the whites lots of wood for the fire."

"I haven't been, no. But I've seen District Six. Flattened. Like a yellow pancake, a few buildings trickling down a gravel hill. At least they left the churches and mosques."

"A ghost town," Ezz said, "so empty and desolate, with the wind blowing through everything. And all those people pushed for nothing into council homes in the Cape Flats. The whites are scared. They know what it meant to us."

Hans nodded. "They say when the Southeaster blows and you drive along Caledon Street and park the car you can hear the banjos and *ghommaliedjies* and the cries of the people who used to live there."

"Shame."

"When they demolished it, they killed the spirit of the

people," Riaana said. "Took away the heart of the Coloureds and Cape Malays."

"I don't like those words."

"What words?"

"Coloureds and Cape Malays. That's their words for us."

"I'm using it for practicality," Riaana said. "What's your word for you?"

"Muslim."

"Or Canadian," Jeff said. "At least you can call yourself that."

"I'm a Canadian citizen, that's all."

"Canada's played a big part helping South Africa," Ezz popped an olive into her mouth. "Arthur, can you bring out the dessert and the bowls?"

"Not like those *kaks* in the White House," Myrna added. "If this was Israel, you would've seen them kick some real arse long ago. They point a finger to show they're cross, but keep their hands on their balls, fucking hypocrites."

"Is it difficult to get into a squatter camp?"

"Damn dangerous. Why?"

"I was thinking of taking a look."

"Taking a look? It's not an amusement park. For what?"

"Don't be so hostile, Myrna," Jeff said. "She's just asking."

"I saw a documentary on television the other day. Seven-year-olds giving their feelings and views. I couldn't believe what I heard."

"You never knew?"

"I didn't know them when I lived here. I never knew how they felt. I couldn't believe a seven-year-old talking about darkness, the darkness of South Africa. Seven years old."

There was an uncomfortable silence.

"You've been away a long time," Hans said.

"And you know what they say about us, the ones in the middle — do you think we could've helped? I mean, we did get it better than them."

"God, I hate this," Myrna plunked down her glass. "Suddenly everyone has a conscience. Next thing you'll tell us you're coming back to help."

"I *am* coming back."

"There. What did I say."

"Not everyone left of their own accord," Riaana said.

"What do you mean?" Ezz asked.

"I don't think Sabah wants to discuss it. And she's always talked of coming back."

"Why?"

"It's home."

"It's dysfunctional."

"Aren't we all children of a dysfunctional womb? You've turned out all right."

"Speak for yourself," Myrna said.

"Hey, hey," Ezz shot her a look. "Sabah's my guest."

"It's all right. I'd feel the same about any born-again, returning South African. But, show me a non-white who hasn't suffered some kind of identity crisis, and I'll show you someone who's bought the plan."

"Maybe. But, *you* didn't take advantage of your white skin? Tell me the oppression *you* felt."

"You know what I think?" Hans asked Ezz.

"What do you think?"

"I think this is turning into one of our famous *beat the visiting Canadian into a corner for running away* fights.

Remember what happened to Chris two months ago? We should stop now. Sabah didn't come to be interrogated."

"It's all right," I said. "But you know what I'm tired of, Myrna?"

"What?"

"I'm tired of this singsong over who's more oppressed. Holding onto it like some coveted award. Let it go, man. Give it air. Black people aren't the only ones. Pain is pain. For anyone who's suffered under this regime. It's not about who suffered the most. We have our own demons to work on, don't think we don't. The middle people have had it better than the black people, yes, but the middle people have suffered too. We can't dwell on and on. At least, if you have a black skin, you know you're black. The devil isn't at your elbow telling you to just get into the white section of the train 'cause there you'll have a seat, or leave out your race on the job ap because you're damn qualified and want the job. Whiteskins are tempted everyday into falseness and deceit. What's *that* a result of? Who do *I* send the bill to for the last forty years? Malan? Verwoerd? De Klerk? Damn right I'm coming back! South Africa belongs to all of us. The last fucker who said that to me, kicked me out. Does that make me a born-again, returning hypocrite? We've all been fucked by apartheid."

"Arthur, dessert!" Ezz shouted, although Arthur was right next to her.

"Shit, Ezz, you don't have to scream in my ear."

"Give Sabah a cigarette."

"I quit."

"A rye and coke."

"I don't drink."

"Well, something then," Ezz said. "And you," turning

to Myrna, "you should listen to people before you open your fat mouth."

"Excuse me? Your foot's still in yours from poking your nose into Gerald's business last week."

"Your *poes*, man."

"Did you see my *poes*?"

"Oh, shut up you. And yes, I did. Start wearing underwear."

"This is how the majority of people feel though, Sabah," Hans said. "Returning South Africans are opportunists. Coming back to ride the wave. To make money, live amongst the rich on Devil's Peak, lording it over their families."

"Not everyone, Hans. Some of us never left. There's prejudice all over, only here they call it apartheid and everyone acts like we invented the disease."

"In Canada, a Canadian citizen can vote," Myrna came back.

"That's true."

"So there're differences."

"Who's arguing? I'm saying, let's move on. If Mandela can show compassion, who the hell are we to suck on the past like an old tit? If we want *them* to change, *we* have to change. It starts in the heart. There's just no point lamenting the past. I'm sorry, man, that's how I see it. Now if I have no voice because I left, well that's emotional, not smart."

"Well, fuck, isn't this whole argument emotional?"

"Oh, for Christ's sake. Would you stop it already?" Ezz knocked her elbow into Myrna's arm.

"Why're you coming back, Sabah?"

"For the smell of the sea."

"Oh, my word."

"For the mist over Table Mountain."

"You're crazy."

"For *sourfig konfyt*. For the hawker with
ing front teeth, shouting, 'Merem, love
H.I.V. positively good!'"

"You *have* romanticized this place."

"I left my soul at the foot of Table Mountain. I want it
back."

Jeff lit another joint. "Ask a stupid fucking question."

"What's this?" Ezz asked. "Everyone's swearing now?
See what you started, Sabah?"

"At least she's laughing," Rollie said. "Here, try a sip of
this. A little brandy's good for you."

"No thanks."

"I understand how she feels," Ezz said. "We take this
place for granted. Look how many times we said we
would leave. Oh fuck, she's crying. Sabah?"

"See what you did?" Jeff accused. "*Jy hou ook nie op nie.
Jy bly moet die Canadians.*"

"Sabah? Do you want to go outside?"

"I'm fine. Just go about your business."

"I'm sorry," Ezz said. "We shouldn't have attacked you
like this."

"You didn't attack me. This is the language I know.
What I miss. Why I want to come back."

"And you will come back, and we'll pick it up from
here. There'll be lots of nights like this. Arthur, did you
make the tea? I think Sabah likes tea."

"*Jy order net*," Arthur mumbled, going back out with
the tray.

Myrna went to the sideboard for a pack of cards.
"Poker, anyone?"

"Strip?" Rollie Thomas asked.

"We stop at the shirt," Ezz said. "None of that non-sense of the last time."

"What's the fun of it then?"

Hans lit a joint, Rollie put out the peanuts and chips.

What had happened this night of strangers and dagga talk? Had my tongue been loosened by the freedom in that room or the backwash in my soul? I returned to the buzz in that room many times when I saw my country's unrest unfold on the screen in my living room.

Sometimes I hear Ezz' laughter and see Hans' hand steal up her thigh, and feel the fires of Africa warm my bones. I stayed, that night, drugged with life, until my clothes reeked of smoke and Myrna was down to her serviette underwear.

❖

GIVE THEM TOO MUCH

CHEEKY, THESE COLOUREDS ARE GETTING, I tell you. Some of them downright cocky since they took down the signs and Clifton looking like wild rice on mash — mealies and blankets and children with soggy diapers right next to where your neighbour's stirring his drink. They don't know how to behave now that they're allowed on our beaches. Give them your finger, and you have an epidemic on your hands.

I do the books at Rolaine's, behind where the designers have their drawing boards and Mr. David sometimes gets his hand snagged in a model's underpants. There're benefits, of course, keeping still and saying nothing while it crawls up your thigh like the Nile into Egypt in search of its wet beginnings — discounts in the showroom, a raise — and most girls just fear for their jobs.

The family's also notorious for their histrionics, raving like cross-eyed hyenas for any little mistake, Mr. David not alone in his harassment of coloured girls, although his brother, Mr. Saul, with the raspberry mole on his nose, offers biscuits before nailing you behind the door. The darkie from the Malay Quarter who'd cried wolf when Mr. Saul slipped his hand down her blouse, and was then told her shorthand sucked and got sacked, was the one to shake them up. Her father appeared at the factory with records from Woodstock Typing School, threatening sexual harassment in a climate where breast brushings and lascivious come-ons were commonplace, and no one gave a damn. Shocked by the confrontation, they offered her back her job. She quit, and had a lawyer's letter sent, tempering Mr. Saul's behaviour for a few months. Cheeky, I said. Next thing you know, they'll think you want them next to you on the train.

I've been with Rolaine's thirty years, I've seen cockroaches decked out in gold, and the Greenbergs are known for their swollen glands. When girls with tuppence to their names accompany Heidi, our head designer, to Paris for fashion shows, I know one of them's played hide-the-zhol. I've also paid gynies' accounts at Medipark for unlisted procedures. Do they think I was born yesterday? The wives aren't blind, of course, but it's easier to pretend ignorance. They come in on Fridays with their beehives preening like old queens to show they're still on the throne, then return to their pedicures and charities, and lunch at the President. I've been a target myself. When my tits were under my chin. But fifty's old for double-breasted dragons in tight underwear lusting after leather bras, although my legs can beat those models' anytime. And who wants an old tongue that's been everywhere? Those tarts were welcome to those drooping balloons and scaly legs.

Still, life's all right if you don't take too seriously all this new unrest sweeping the country since de Klerk lost his mind. South Africa's managed for three hundred years and isn't going to crumble just because the man's been too long in the sun. They couldn't possibly be serious

about a monkey for a president, and the vote for everyone.

After depositing my pay on Friday afternoons, I visit
Esther Moen up in Vredehoek, and we sit on the verandah overlooking the harbour drinking gin and talking
about our children living overseas. Hers in Madrid, my
Colin and Glenda in the U.K. Children today don't have
the same loyalties.

"I'm sorry, Mom," Glenda had said when she and her
husband broke the news that they were emigrating. "We
don't want to raise our children in this environment."

"But this is *your* environment. You have all the benefits."

At least Glenda writes, and Colin calls every three
months. Not Esther's children. Esther's had a rough time.
Both boys homosexuals — gays they call them now.
What the hell was gay about one man licking another's
private parts? She had to be glad they were out of her
sight, frolicking in Spain. It had to be a helluva jolt dis-
covering a vibrator the size of your arm in your son's
chest of drawers.

To Esther, bad things came all at once. She used to be
a beauty in her day, but when she lost that glow, she also
lost her husband, Jake, to a waitress at the Nelson Inn. A
lot of this seems to be going on. Thank God, my Harry
just died of a stroke.

When Esther starts to get maudlin after too much gin,
I take the bus to my bachelor flat where I call Mavis to
see if she's free to take in a flick. Mavis and I know each
other since high school, and despite what she's done to
herself, I still like her company. When her husband left
five years ago for a girl in a training bra, Mavis had such
a collapse, she left for Europe for three months to give

herself a lift. She returned with lotions and salts, a new face, marble tits, and a wolfishness for young boys. When I saw that first stud with the bulging crotch open the door of her MG in front of Charlie C's, I knew Mavis was paying for it.

I *am* lonesome for a nice gentleman caller though. A funny thing happens to a woman after fifty. There's that terrible stretch looming, and one has to put by, along with the pension, a little male companionship just in case. I've no intention ending up one of those rinsed blue-heads walking my randy poodle on the boardwalk. But then that's the rub with a job like mine, cooped up with trial balances in the back room, your only male contacts the driver, teaboy, cutters, and sewing-machine mechanics.

Still, they all come to me with their tales of woe.

"Mrs. B," Mr. David said to me the other day, "I want you to talk to Danny. He's been getting cheeky with those Merriweather people again, just got a call from the manager."

"Why don't you lay him off for a week to teach him a lesson?"

"He's got six children, don't be daft. Speak to him, and tell him to keep his mouth in check."

And if it isn't Mr. David or Mr. Saul, it's the machinists or one of the girls. Do I have a sticker on my forehead saying I'm the Complaints Bureau? I don't think so. Although I must say I like being Mother Superior to some of them. When Melvin rolls in the tea trolley, I always ask about his crippled son. I'm not one for snubbing them like that English snot up in the front talking to buyers on the telephone in that phony accent.

I'm friendly with all of them, particularly the designers. Except for Heidi, who's German, and Pamela, who's like me, they are all Muslim. Coming from families of tailors and dressmakers, they have a knack for pattern making and design. And some of them — now I'd never say this out loud because if there's one thing you learn in a place like this, it's that a non-white must never be compliment-ed to his face — but some of them, I swear, are more gen-uine than whites. Except I could never figure that new one they hired last year.

It wasn't that Hala Baker was rude or impolite, but she had an aloofness that grated on me. On tea breaks while she would offer you a biscuit or sweet from her tin, she never joined in when we talked about the Greenbergs and their little liaisons, and wasn't at all like the others trying to ingratiate herself.

I was in the backroom sorting accounts that cold Tuesday afternoon Mr. David came sniffing around the design room for a feel. The wall's just a thin partition, and I knew the others were out on the floor, Hala the only one there. I strained my ears, but couldn't hear any-thing. Just when I had my fingers poised over the adding machine, there was her voice, "Mr. David, I'm sorry!" in a tone I'd never heard before, seconds later, Mr. David, acting like someone badly frightened by the unexpected ferocity of a puppy dog, storming out in a snit.

It was obvious what he'd tried and, when the others came back, I had my ear pressed to the wall. But Hala Baker mentioned nothing of the incident that would've livened up the tea break, given her status. I envied her that control — an arrogance you'll find with a lot of them. They're staunch, I'll give them that. The worst one'll fast during the holy month. But they have a pride, especially on Fridays when they get two hours for lunch to attend mosque and during Ramadan. They'll sit there with their parched lips and stiff smiles showing you how your biscuits and tea don't affect them at all, and you just know they think they're closer to God. Would God have given this land to the white man if they were the chosen ones? Once I made a batch of apricot tarts for a kitchen tea for one of them and the girl had the temerity to ask if I'd used lard. As if I didn't know their rule about bacon and pork. I tell you, cut them some slack, and they're like gorillas in a banana tree.

Not long after this incident with Mr. David, Heidi told me Hala was getting married in Woodstock Town Hall, and had invited all of them. I hadn't even known she was engaged. Secretive, I thought. Sweet on top, but probably the kind that when you lifted up the toaster, you'd find a month's crumbs underneath.

Muslims give fairy tale weddings, spending ridiculous amounts on flower girls, page boys, horse-drawn carriages, several costume-changes in one afternoon, and I knew the reception would be a lavish affair. Marnie had gotten married the previous year — don't ask me how he managed it on a cutter's wage — and stories of tables groaning with legs of lamb, chicken breyani, and steak *sosaati* still conjure up pictures of great Cape Malay delights. I thought longingly of how I'd look in my green silk dress.

But Hala Baker hadn't invited me.

"I'm going to the shop, Mrs. B," Melvin came limping in a few minutes before lunch. "You want anything?"

"Which shop are you going to?"

"Danny's giving me an' Miss Heidi a lift to Adderley Street. She's buying de present an' de card for everyone to sign. I also have to buy my own."

"Your own?"

"A person can't go empty-handed, mos. My wife awready bought de doilies."

"I see. I can't believe Danny's so generous giving you a lift on his lunchtime."

Melvin laughed, "Dat's 'cause he's too lazy to go into the shop himself. An' a lousy five rand he gives for a present, troo's Gawd. What can you buy for five rand?"

I was stunned. The crippled teaboy and the insolent driver and not me. Didn't she know who I was? That even Heidi came to me when the Greenbergs needed softening for a promotion she wanted to try?

But I never let on I was miffed. I still joined them on the break. Most days, though, I got indigestion from the freshness in that room. Heidi would pour Hala's tea, and they'd talk about the play at the Nico Malan and act like they'd all played marbles together as children. Like you could sit with a *kaffir* and not notice he's stuffing chips into a loaf of bread and dunking it in his tea. The Germans, we all knew, were encouraged to come and lighten things up, have quite a bent for dark meat, and there were plenty stories of Heidi's skirts-up with coloured men.

A week before the wedding, an announcement over the speakers summoned everyone to the main floor and, with the three hundred rand collected, Heidi presented Hala with a tea set. There were biscuits and speeches, and I stood there grinning like a meerkat, amazed at the lavishness of the gift. My wedding present thirty years ago — of course there'd only been ten of us then — had been a satin nightie in tissue wrap, and here a girl who hadn't been at Rolaine's long enough to get used to the soft paper in the front toilet was the recipient of a magnificent tea set. Why was it so necessary to prove ourselves? Probably a white designer with ten months' service would've gotten a lace tablecloth.

"Hala, can you come with me a minute, please?", Mr. Saul asked the designer when everything was over and workers returned to their posts.

I had to pick up the orders from Miss Rathbone in the front, and followed at a reasonable distance, watching Hala enter the corner office with Mr. Saul.

Miss Rathbone hadn't attended the presentation and was on the telephone speaking to a buyer. I pointed to the folder on the desk. She could've handed it to me, but made me wait until she'd finished a speech about the popularity of ostrich feather trim. Just as well.

Looking around at the samples hanging against the wall, I heard a commotion next door. Then the door flew open, Hala rushed out, words spittling out of Mr. Saul's mouth.

"Miss Baker, I didn't —"

He didn't know we were there and charged by Rathbone's cardboard booth. At the front desk he caught up with her and grabbed her arm. Then a curious thing happened. As I say time and time again, but no one listens any more — give them too much, and this is what you can expect. Hala stopped, grabbed the sugar bowl from the secretary's tea tray, and flung its grainy contents into the guts of the IBM typewriter on the desk. She ran past the receptionist, out the door, and was gone.

The audacity of the girl!

When all the talk had died down and life droned on to the strings of some new symphony over the buzzing noise of machines — for the story did make the rounds — I was going through my accounts-payable folder one afternoon when I found, stuck between two overdue accounts, a gold-edged invitation neatly addressed to Mrs. B.

❖

MAKE THE CHICKEN RUN

THE COLD BIT INTO HER EARS, numbing them. She would never get used to this weather, never. She locked the car, the wind grazing her skin, and walked up to the doors of the school.

... One is shaped by one's environment, the saying goes. But what happens when you take a rhino out of the veldt and put him in a cage?

The emotional damage of apartheid is large. It clogs the pores, deadens the heart. We have seen the afterclap of setting people apart. The rage. And in this melee over rights and land and being the chosen race, everyone's forgotten the apricot-skinned hunter whose footprints first tracked the shores of the Cape of Good Hope. Thousands of years before Van Riebeeck came. Before the blacks. Before the whites. Where is the Bushman now? Does it matter who came first?

I can't find the words to express what I feel at the compassion of the next man who will be president. Such a lack of bitterness. Such grace. How is it possible? But then, you're a great man, too. Brave. You could've waited three more years, ten. More people could've died; more will. Of course, you are also a clever man.

Blood was staining the flag, the sanctions were gutting your nuts, you had to harness your balls. To me, setting Nelson Mandela free was your greatest achievement in life.

But there're old griefs, old hurts that in the winter months come to haunt me with force. November's the worst time. Naked trees under weepy skies, the landscape draped in grey.

Do you know a country can make one cry? I have an unhealthy passion for it, they say. But, then it's easy for outsiders to judge. What do they know of my land? Of its smells? You cannot be sown in wildness and settle amongst daffodils.

When I was sixteen I wanted to go to business college and got a white card. I thought you could change your identity and escape who you were. Just change the C to a W and get a new life. I got a new life all right. And a new country. And a whole new loneliness. I'd committed a serious crime — the sentence, banishment. Nothing crude like taking me by my neck to the boat, but what does it matter how the message was conveyed?

Living in exile is hard. A South African going home for a holiday doesn't tell the truth. He can't afford to let on. He keeps up the show, promotes his new home. The freedom and opportunities. But he's not free in his soul. The first thing that hits you in a new country is the loneliness. You'd rather be with old friends in someone's kitchen sharing a pan of snoek *than in a fancy apartment overlooking a lake, getting fifty extra bucks in your pay. It's less important now, that seat on the train. Your whole body cries out for just a whiff of the flowersellers on the parade.*

Of course, not all South Africans feel this way. Some are here because they want to be here. They've gone on with their lives, carved new niches in Canada's rich tapestry. Some have chosen to forget. Some even avoid other South Africans. A family who didn't have a mat on their living room floor in Athlone in 1968, now, in their monster mansion, have no dealings with fellow Capetonians. With housekeepers, mortgages, cognac over fireside chats with the right-coloured friends, they have it down at last.

Then there're the ones who skimmed the cream till the milk thinned, and when it looked like they would have to give some of it back, ran, came here, and practise the same bullshit at Bayview and Steeles. They haven't changed. They haven't even developed the art of disguise.

"Where did you live in Cape Town?"

"Why don't you just ask what I am?"

They're not used to responses like this and, out of guilt, accept my invitation to lunch. I feed them roast chicken with butternut squash, then, over trifle, ask what action they took to help the blacks, feeling as sorry for them as they did. It wasn't enough just to talk. What did they do? They can't leave my house fast enough, afterwards avoiding me like a locust storm. I only met one, a railway worker, who said, "Hell, man, the blecks are gonna take over. I didn't wanna be there when those Zulus ran into town."

My grandfather had a strange saying, **whenever you take a fish out of water, it's wet.**

Some things remain the same.

A new country is hard for anyone — especially one with so many cultures, languages, traditions not your own. Do you know, parents here work themselves into the ground, children carry appointment books? At least at home kids can still enjoy a good, barefooted roll in the sand and play kennetjie until dark. Or is it cowboys and crooks with AK-47s now?

The reality is, the people left. And South Africa let them go. The devil done rise his ugly head and make the chicken run!

My trouble with the law may have started with that card, but resentment began when I was in diapers. I had the audacity to come out white. White is good. White is right. White gets you everything. It got me a phone call to the C.I.D. from someone in the family. Can hatred go deeper?

Still, South Africa was home. I knew its secrets, loved its noises and smells, was part of the smoke of the land. It was hard putting roots down on the other side of the world. The crushing cold, the bleached emptiness. No magic, no flavour, no pulse.

When my son was born, I went home for a holiday, and was shocked by how strange everything appeared. After the open spaces of Canada, the roads seemed narrow and small, attitudes hadn't changed, too many things rushed at me. But in no time I was used to its clamour and cries, and felt that insatiable aliveness I knew so well. Too soon, though, I had to say goodbye, saving my tears for over the Karoo, away from prying eyes. When I arrived in Toronto to freezing rain, snow, clogged highways, I asked God what crime I'd committed to receive such a harsh penalty. He didn't answer in those days. Or maybe I wasn't listening. In the middle lane of the 401, going a hundred and ten, I opened the door to jump. My husband drove straight to Emergency. Emergency is a busy place. Accident victims, head injuries, heart attacks. Attempted suicides are a drain on a physician's time. The doctor spent half an hour trying to decide whether I was a danger to myself, then advised a one-way ticket home.

Six months of therapy after that. I couldn't watch anything on television to do with my country. I blocked it out, practised selective blindness with that first wave of riots and the state of emergency. But I couldn't escape. Suddenly South Africa was on the map, and we got wind of all its farts. There was a new aware- ness, curiosity, everyone waking up to injustices old as the hills, hungry for facts. Just because I was South African they thought I knew what went on.

I watched with a new intensity. I saw for the first time my black brothers and sisters. I didn't know them in 1968. They were not on my street, not in my school, not in my thoughts. But I watched now, through the smoke and the tear gas, and was ashamed that the middle children have had it better than them.

My first years as an immigrant were wild. I had a dangerous

intensity. Someone always paid, usually those closest to me.

"There's no religion in Canada," people said when I left. "You already don't know who you are." But it was here, in the hard, white bleakness, God heard my cries. And when He did, I rebelled. There were lessons still to be learned.

I once tried to kidnap my kids, little considering that Canada was their home, where they were born. In my unhappiness, I was going to displace them as I had been displaced. Luckily, I was stopped.

After the divorce, I gave up on humans, bought a parrot, and called him Hendrik. Six months of training, but finally the parrot got it right. Every morning I would come into the kitchen, say, "Morning Hendrik," and Hendrik would launch into his routine, "Sorry, Sabah. Sorry Sabah." All day long. Whenever it saw me. Especially when I had guests. "Sorry, Sabah" in that monotone. Not long after Hendrik mastered this art, he made the mistake of coming out of his cage when Kafifi was two hours late getting her salmon deluxe, and I arrived home to yellow feathers on the couch, Kafifi curled up in the corner licking her whiskers, immensely satisfied. After a decent period of mourning, I replaced Hendrik with a green-tipped meanie called Pik, spent hours chanting, "Amandla, Amandla," but the damn bird just gave me that hooded look, and wouldn't say anything.

Shortly after the state of emergency I had an appointment with a family of Jamaicans to list their property. The wife picked up an accent and asked if I was South African.

"Yes," I replied.

"White?"

"No" I said, continuing with my pitch. Halfway through, she stopped me.

"I'm sorry, I don't believe you're not a white South African. I can't do business with you."

The husband tried to fix things, but I didn't want her talked into dealing with me. It was a slap in the face, being rebuffed for something I wasn't guilty of, the irony of it; yet I felt bolstered that she'd taken a stand. I know other South Africans with strong accents working in sales who tell their clients they're English.

Not long ago, I met a sculptor who'd showed her work all over the world. She was in Toronto for two weeks, and for an hour I listened to her fascinating tales. Somewhere between the shrimp and dessert, she slipped in that she was South African. There hadn't been a trace of an accent. Trying not to look surprised, I replayed our conversation to see if I'd said anything out of place, and was glad that for once I hadn't scratched that old sore. But it was a lesson for me. Especially, at the end, when without malice, passing the cream, she asked, "Do you think that, quite possibly, Sabah, you might be a racist?"

Apartheid's like heart disease. We're all casualties, we all have our goggas in the dark, our prejudices. It's going to take an understanding of the disease to reverse the damage.

Finally, we come to the country that healed my wounds and gave me back my self-esteem. I came to love it at last, its generosity. Canada's warmed up with the different colours of the world since I first came, I look at it differently now. I'm proud to say I live here. I'm proud to say, now, "O Canada, I stand on guard for thee," for it did stand watch over me.

My children are grown now. Proud Canadians. They tell me I've done a good job. If I want to leave, they'll understand. But now that I can, I can't. I guess the jay's wings have caught just too many times on the fence. I've gotten used to other noises, other smells.

So, here we are, on the lip of change. You're going on to become a great man in history, I've come to terms with myself. If God can forgive and Mandela has no bitterness, who am I to hold out?

The bill is cancelled, Mr. President.

The room was hot, crowded. The red-and-white flag a sharp reminder, reviving another time, another banner, Table Mountain receding in the distance. Where had the time gone? How had she changed that she was standing here with snow in her boots and a pen in her hand? Had she given up or grown up? Her eyes misted, and she hardened herself. She couldn't look a fool in front of these people. Most of them like her. From other countries, other flags. What did tonight mean to them? Had it taken them twenty-seven years to get here?

"Aah, here it is, Sabah Solomon," the lady with the maple-leaf brooch sighed, finding the name in the register. "In there, dear. Don't forget your ballot."

❖

OTHER BOOKS FROM SECOND STORY PRESS